GRAVE DANGER

A MADDIE GRAVES MYSTERY BOOK 12

LILY HARPER HART

HARPERHART PUBLICATIONS

Copyright © 2018 by Lily Harper Hart

All rights reserved.

No part of this book may be reproduced in any form or by any electronic or mechanical means, including information storage and retrieval systems, without written permission from the author, except for the use of brief quotations in a book review.

✾ Created with Vellum

1. ONE

"What are you doing, love?"

Nick Winters furrowed his brow as he stood in the shade of a large maple tree and watched his girlfriend – the woman who would become his wife and was already the whole of his heart – as she prepared herself for a new adventure.

Maddie Graves, her honey blond hair pulled back in a loose braid at the nape of her neck, tugged a wide hat over her serious brow and fixed Nick with a look that was supposed to be stern, but he found adorable.

"I'm gardening."

Nick ran his tongue over his teeth as he surveyed the pile of items she'd secured from the store the previous day. They sat on the ground as she shifted from one foot to the other and swished her hips in a way that caused his lips to curve. "I know," he said after a beat. "You told me the news when you got back from the gardening center yesterday and your entire car was full of stuff that I didn't recognize – stuff that I unloaded without complaint because I'm strong and dashing, mind you. It's just ... why are you going to garden?"

Maddie's face remained blank. "Why wouldn't I want to garden?"

Nick wasn't sure how to answer. In many ways, Maddie was easygoing and never put up much of a fuss. In other ways, she turned high maintenance at the oddest of times. They'd been best friends for their entire lives – other than a ten-year period of estrangement that nearly killed them both – and they'd only been lovers for about nine months. Still, Nick felt he knew Maddie better than anyone.

He didn't know what to make of this new development, though.

"But I don't understand," Nick hedged, his eyes darting from the overgrown flowerbed at the front of the house to his beloved. "You've never shown much interest in gardening before."

Maddie merely shrugged. "I'm going to change that. I bought gloves ... and little hand tools ... and seeds and stuff. It's spring, so now is the time to plant."

"But ... do you know anything about gardening?"

"I looked up some stuff on the internet and they even have a television channel about gardening so I can get ideas."

"They also have a television channel for porn but ... ."

Maddie offered up an expression that was halfway between rueful and annoyed. "Only you would bring up porn when I'm about to embark on a new hobby. That's just so ... you."

Nick leaned closer. "I didn't mean that the way it came out. It's just ... you've never expressed an interest in gardening before and I have no idea what to make of it. Is this some sort of late-twenties crisis?"

"Why do you have to make anything of it?" Maddie wasn't normally known for being aggressive, but the look she shot Nick now was worrisome. "Can't I simply want to pick up a new hobby?"

Nick wasn't sure how to answer. "I think we got off on the wrong foot here." He was uncomfortable, something he almost never felt when spending time with Maddie. "I just want to know why you've decided to start gardening. I don't want to turn it into a big thing."

Maddie opened her mouth to answer but no explanation came out. She was genuinely at a loss. That's when her grandmother stepped in and made things even more awkward.

"Maddie is getting married," Maude Graves drawled from the open doorway, a mug of coffee clutched in her hand and her silver curls still damp from a shower. The expression on her face was mischievous.

Nick glanced over his shoulder and met Maude's steady gaze. "I know she's getting married. I was there when she got the ring."

Maude didn't so much as twitch. "Yes, but now Maddie needs to do wifely things. Gardening is a wifely thing."

Nick blinked several times in rapid succession. "But ... ."

Maude, who generally enjoyed messing with her granddaughter and Nick rather than helping, took pity on the man she'd known since he was a small boy. He was genuinely lost. "She's getting married and it's a wife's job to keep up the house," Maude offered helpfully. "That's what she's doing. She's keeping up the house so you'll be happy."

Understanding dawned on Nick, and it wasn't a comfortable experience. "Maddie." He made a clucking sound with his tongue as he shook his head. "You don't have to garden to make me happy, Mad. In fact, if you never want to garden and instead spend your time kissing me, I will be forever happy."

Maddie offered up a chagrined smile. "Nicky, that's very sweet." She meant it. "That's not why I'm gardening, though."

Nick stilled, his handsome face thoughtful. "So ... you're not gardening because you think that's what a wife does?"

Maddie's answer was perfunctory. "No."

Nick couldn't help being relieved. "Good. That makes me feel better."

"I'm gardening because that's what my mother would want," Maddie added, only adding to Nick's confusion.

"Wait ... what?" Nick glanced to Maude for help, but the Graves matriarch looked as confused as he felt. "You've decided to pick up gardening because your mother liked to garden? I don't ... um ... understand."

"That makes two of us." Maude was suddenly serious. "Maddie girl, your mother gardened because she always liked it." She shuffled out onto the front porch so Maddie had no choice but to meet her steady gaze. "Even when your mother was a kid she used to enjoy picking flowers and weeding the garden. I never made her do those things. She liked it. She said it was relaxing.

"At first I thought she was defective and couldn't understand how a child of mine could possibly like something so ... mundane," she continued. "Then I realized that was the wrong opinion to have. I've always been a big proponent of being who you are ... and your mother happened to like gardening. That's who she was."

Nick was careful to keep his expression neutral. "You don't have to garden, love."

"The beds are overgrown, though," Maddie pointed out, gesturing toward what could only be described as a pile of dead weeds (thanks to the brutal Michigan winter), which looked to be choking what had once been a pretty bush. "When my mother lived here, the beds were beautiful. The flowers were so pretty people all over town commented on how nice they looked."

"Yes, but you're getting married to the town stud," Maude noted. "The people in town have better things to gossip about now, like the fact that you two are so pretty together that everyone else appears ugly when they stand next to you."

Nick snorted. "While I wouldn't exactly put it like that ... ."

Maude cut him off. "Maddie, you don't have to garden to make Olivia happy."

Olivia Graves, Maddie's mother, died almost a year before. It was sudden and traumatic. It was also the thing that forced Maddie back to Blackstone Bay, a small hamlet in northern Lower Michigan, and resulted in Maddie and Nick reuniting. Even though the initial meeting was tense, Maddie and Nick found their way back to one another fairly quickly and once they were a couple it was as if everything slipped into place and their future was set in stone. Oddly enough, they were both fine with that. The only thing Maddie and Nick believed with absolute certainty was that they belonged together.

Forever.

"I know I don't have to garden to make Mom happy." Maddie's

tone was firm. "We've talked about it and she said that the house was mine and I could do what I want with the flowerbeds."

Olivia may have been dead, but her ghost remained to offer up advice and admonishments. Since Maddie was the only one who could see and talk to ghosts, those motherly musings didn't fall on deaf ears and no one else could ease the burden of Olivia's chats because they couldn't participate in them.

"I gave it some serious thought and I want to put the gardens back to what they were before," Maddie said. "I'm not doing it for Mom. I'm doing it for me."

"But why?" Nick desperately wanted to understand. "You've never cared before."

"I know but ... ." Maddie searched for the correct words to make Nick not only understand but also refrain from worrying. "I love this house and I love what my mother did with the flower beds. I remember seeing the house from afar when I was a kid and I was coming home after we spent a day in the woods or getting ice cream, Nicky, and I always loved the flower beds because they were the first thing I saw when we rounded the corner on the street."

Nick licked his lips, uncertain. "So you want to clean up the flower beds because you loved them?"

Maddie nodded. "Yes. I want our children to look at the house the same way I did. I want them to be happy to come home."

Nick smiled and this time the expression was easy and made it all the way up to his eyes. "I think that sounds like a fine idea."

Maddie beamed. "Good. I'm going to need your help to do it. You should probably change your clothes."

Nick balked. "Hey, I don't want to garden."

"No, and I have no intention of making you do it long term." Maddie adopted a "no nonsense" tone that Nick was becoming familiar with. He mostly enjoyed it when she got bossy because it didn't regularly happen. It was often a spur-of-the-moment thing. She clearly meant business now, though. "I let it go for a full year and that's too long of a time. See those weeds over there." Maddie pointed for emphasis. "They're as tall as I am and I'm going to need help yanking them."

"Oh." Nick stared at the weed in question. It did look rather unruly. Since it was early spring in Michigan, the flowers and foliage hadn't yet taken full bloom. "Now would probably be the time to remove that sucker, huh?"

Maddie nodded. "It will take a bit of muscle to get things back to where they were, but if we work together, it will be done quickly and it won't be nearly as much work next year because we'll be keeping it up."

"And this is important to you?"

Maddie bobbed her head. "We're going to start a family here. I want this house to be beautiful, exactly how I remember it from when I was a kid. I know it sounds corny, but I can't stop myself from wanting it."

Nick's expression softened. "Love, I want that, too." He took a step toward her and tipped up her chin with his thumb, planting a long kiss on her lips. "I'll change my clothes and grab some gloves. I think we also need some of those big lawn and leaf bags."

"There are some in the shed behind the house," Maddie said, her eyes already on the flower bed. "If we work together, it won't take us very long."

"That's good. That means we can play together later tonight, right?" Nick's tone was impish, but his eyes offered up a hint of seriousness.

"Absolutely." Maddie liked both ideas.

"Then that sounds like a plan to me."

NICK SPENT TEN minutes changing his clothes and gathering the necessary supplies. He ran into Maude in the backyard after gathering the appropriate bags and pulled up short when he gauged the expression on her face.

"Oh, don't make things difficult," Nick groused. "Everything is fine. There's no reason to be ... well, you."

If Maude was offended by the comment, she didn't show it. "I'm not saying things aren't fine. I simply wanted to touch base with you."

Nick was taken aback – and mildly chagrined. "Oh, well, what seems to be the problem then?"

"I just wanted to tell you that you did a good job handling that." Maude was very rarely serious so Nick couldn't refrain from being flabbergasted. "You two are having fewer and fewer misunderstandings these days and things seem to be falling into place."

Nick narrowed his eyes, suspicious. "Okay, what do you want?"

Maude's face flashed with annoyance. "What makes you think I want anything?"

"I've met you." Nick refused to back down. "You're clearly up to something."

"That's a terrible thing to say about the woman who used to babysit you," Maude shot back. "I mean ... I took care of you, cooked for you, baked for you, entertained you ... and this is how you repay me, huh?" She made a tsking sound with her tongue. "You're breaking my heart."

Nick refused to be swayed. "You never did any of those things for me. Olivia did those things for me. You didn't do anything but try to point me toward mischief. Okay, you entertained me. You didn't bake and cook, though."

"I could've done those things," Maude pressed.

"And yet you didn't."

"No, but I could have."

"But you didn't."

Maude made an exaggerated face. "Do we really need to get fixated on this?"

Nick was genuinely fond of Maude – so much so he considered her a part of his family even when he and Maddie were estranged – so he knew how to play the game. "No. We don't. I have a feeling Maddie is going to be a taskmaster this afternoon so I actually want to get work done rather than play with you. Why don't you tell me what you're doing out here, huh?"

"I would be glad to." Maude almost looked serene. "You can't let

Maddie dig up that flower bed on the east side of the house until at least tomorrow."

The simple statement was the last thing Nick expected. "The one under the garage window?"

"The one under my apartment window," Maude clarified. Several months before she converted the garage into a living space so she could avoid climbing stairs while giving Maddie and Nick privacy at the same time. "You need to keep Maddie away from that flower bed until I can ... deal with things."

Since he was a police officer, Nick wasn't sure he wanted further details. "Do I even want to know?"

Maude was a master at feigning innocence. "Know what?"

"What you're hiding in the flower bed beneath your bedroom window."

"Oh, *that*." Maude made a dramatic face. "What makes you think I'm hiding anything there?"

"Do you really want to play this game?" Nick wasn't in the mood to be trifled with. "Whatever you've got out there – and I've decided I don't want to know, so you're getting off lucky, quite frankly – I want you to get rid of it because I'm guessing it's going to upset Maddie."

"I'm not saying I have anything out there," Maude clarified. "I need you to know that."

Nick's tone was dry. "Duly noted."

"I just think it would be better if you could keep Maddie away from that window until tomorrow," Maude clarified. "I think that for her mental health – and yours as well – that it would be the best thing for everybody."

Now Nick was certain he didn't want to know what Maude was up to. He'd been down that road before and always lived to regret it. That didn't mean he was willing to kowtow to Maude's whims. "You have an hour."

Maude balked. "Excuse me?"

"You have an hour," Nick repeated. "Get rid of it. Whatever it is, I don't want to see it. If it's illegal and I see you with it, I'm going to arrest you."

Maude was agitated but she didn't believe that threat for a second. "Whatever. You're not going to arrest me because it would upset Maddie and we both know you don't want that."

"I don't," Nick agreed, shoving the bags under his arm and starting for the side of the house. "I want her happy."

"Which is why you're gardening." Maude's manner was derisive. "You're all about making her happy."

"You say that like it's a bad thing." Despite Maude's determination to irritate him, Nick picked an easy pace so the elderly woman would have no problem keeping up. "I want Maddie happy. I'm not going to pretend otherwise."

"Well, if that's true, you'll keep her away from the flower bed on the other side of the house until at least tomorrow."

Nick heaved out a sigh. "You are so much work."

"Yes, but I'm worth it." Maude's eyes twinkled in a way that made Nick smile. "Just keep her busy until I give you the go-ahead to hit that flower bed. It won't be that difficult."

Nick was resigned. "I'll see what I can do. Make sure I don't see whatever you've got in there, though. I'd like to at least pretend I'm a good cop."

"You're the best cop I know." Maude was serious. "You've never arrested me."

"Well, I'll put that at the top of my résumé should I need to find another job thanks to your hijinks."

"That's a good word," Maude noted. "*Hijinks*. Maybe I'll start a new club with that word in the title. I like it."

"I'm more than just a pretty face." Nick was grinning when he rounded the final corner and found Maddie kneeling in front of the flower beds, an intense look on her face and a small rake in her hand. "Man, she is really beautiful." He didn't intend to say the words out loud, but they escaped. "Look how cute she is because she's so focused."

Maude rolled her eyes. "You guys are way too sweet. You give me indigestion."

"You'll live. In fact ... ." Whatever Nick was about to say died on his lips as Maddie went rigid, her body snapping to attention as her head lolled to the side. "What the ... ?"

Sensing his worry, Maude swiveled quickly and frowned. "What's happening?"

"I don't know." Nick took a long stride forward. "Maddie?"

Instead of focusing on him, Maddie's eyes rolled back in her head and she tilted and fell to the ground. At that exact moment, the phone in her pocket started trilling. Nick ignored that as he dropped the bags he carried and broke into a run.

He could only think of one thing. He only cared about one thing.

"Maddie!"

2. TWO

Maddie's mind was a jumble.

One second she was trying to decide which weeds she wanted to pull first and the second all she could hear was screaming. At first she thought it was coming from someplace behind her; perhaps Mrs. Northrup's house a block down was the source of the noise. Then she realized the screaming was coming from her mind and things were so much worse.

The images flashing through her busy brain were hard to grasp. A woman running through the darkness, blond hair streaming behind her as a shadow gave chase. Another woman, this one slightly older but with the same blond hair, backing away from a menacing figure. Blood. Tears. Overwhelming sobs and screams.

All of it converged at once and Maddie thought for sure her circuits were going to overload, that something in her brain was readying itself to blow. Then she heard something else, something soothing, and she latched onto the sound because she knew otherwise she would be completely lost.

"Maddie."

Nicky. Maddie thought she said his name, but instinctively she knew she felt it rather than uttered it.

"Love, please ... ." Nick's voice cracked as Maddie's eyelids fluttered.

It took everything she had, but when Maddie forced open her eyes she found Nick's anguished brown orbs trained on her face while Maude struggled to keep her hands from shaking as she played with her phone.

"Maddie?" Nick's voice came out in a whoosh when he realized she was awake. "Baby, are you okay? I ... look at me."

Maddie could look nowhere else. She wanted to lose herself in the angular planes of his face rather than the images stalking the edges of her mind. "Nicky." This time she managed to get the single word out, although it was a struggle. "Nicky."

"You scared the crap out of me." Nick cradled Maddie against him, gardening tools discarded and forgotten as he rocked her back and forth. "I thought ... ." He didn't finish. He didn't want to give voice to the thought.

"I'm calling 911," Maude offered. "We'll have help here soon."

Maddie struggled to regain her senses, but Maude's words bored inside and she was present enough to stop her grandmother before she placed a call no one wanted to explain. "No. I don't need an ambulance."

Nick balked. "You most certainly do. You fainted."

"I didn't faint." Maddie hated that word. It was so ... weak.

"Your eyes rolled back in your head and you were out for at least thirty seconds, Mad," Nick argued. "You're going to the hospital."

"No, I'm not." Maddie managed to be firm, but just barely. "I'm fine."

"You fainted," Nick challenged.

"I didn't faint ... and I don't like that word." Maddie struggled to sit, but Nick kept her plastered to his chest. He was so strong she couldn't find the energy to push him back, so ultimately she relented and remained where she was. "I'm fine. I just ... lost myself for a moment."

Nick didn't like the sound of that one bit. "And how did you lose yourself?"

That right there was a tricky question. "Well ... ." Her phone started ringing again, causing her eyes to snap down to her pocket. "Oh."

"Do you know who that is?" Nick's eyebrows migrated north. "Your phone started ringing right as it happened. I ... you ... I mean ... ." Nick pressed his eyes shut as he fought to calm himself. She was alive. She was conscious and present. She was with him. Everything would be okay. He was certain of it.

"So am I calling an ambulance or not?" Maude asked, confused.

"Yes," Nick answered immediately.

"Absolutely not!" Maddie shot her grandmother a warning look. "Don't even think about it. I'm fine." She dug for her phone, frowning when the ringing stopped. "I missed him again. He's going to think it's on purpose."

"Who is going to think it's on purpose?" Nick didn't view himself as histrionic but he was drifting very close to the edge of a meltdown. "Maddie, what is going on?"

"It's Dwight." Maddie licked her lips as she smiled at the mention of her Detroit police officer friend. He was one of the few people she maintained contact with when she left Detroit. "He wants to talk to me."

Nick wasn't sure what to make of Maddie's matter-of-fact nature. "Why? What does he want from you?"

Maddie balked at his tone. "He's a friend. Perhaps he simply wants to talk." Even as she said the words, Maddie knew they weren't true. The images she saw in her head, even though she didn't realize it at the time, were clearly from a big city. Dwight worked the mean and often violent streets of Detroit. It made sense that she was overwhelmed by the visions at the same time her phone rang. The visions were tied to Dwight.

Nick stared into Maddie's face for what felt like forever. "Do you believe that?"

He was putting her on the spot and they both knew it. "I ... ." Maddie didn't get a chance to answer because Nick's phone started ringing.

Nick shifted so he could retrieve his iPhone. When looked at the display screen, he wasn't surprised to find Dwight listed as the contact.

"That's for me." Maddie instinctively reached for the phone, but Nick shook his head and pressed the button to answer before greeting Dwight in the most nonchalant manner he could muster.

"What's up?"

Maddie watched, her eyes wide as Nick calmly shifted so he could get comfortable on the ground. He kept one arm around her so she couldn't escape his grasp and she made a face when she was forced to listen rather than participate in the conversation.

"How are things?" Dwight asked. He was clearly on edge. Nick didn't know the man well, but he recognized that.

"For the most part, they're great," Nick replied. "Maddie and I are engaged."

"I know. She called right after Christmas, bubbling with excitement and crying."

"Crying?" Nick slid a look to Maddie. "You cried when you told him you were marrying the man of your dreams?"

Maddie merely shrugged. "They were happy tears at the time. I feel like crying right now for a different reason."

"I can see that." Nick absently patted the hand resting on her midriff and focused on the conversation. "Despite the tears, Dwight, I kept my promise. I'm keeping her happy ... er, at least for the most part. We're gardening and everything."

"That sounds like an old fogey thing to do." Dwight did his best to hold up his end of the conversation without pushing too fast. Nick grasped the signs and part of him wanted to take pity on the obviously distressed police detective. The other part – the part that recognized something very bad was about to happen – wanted to hang up and block Dwight's number.

"Well, we're old fogeys at heart," Nick said evenly. "How are things with you? How is Sage?"

Several months before, in a fit of despair, Dwight visited Maddie for help because his college-aged daughter went missing. Maddie insisted on helping and after several days, they managed to track down the girl and reunite her with Dwight. Maddie and Dwight had been talking on the phone every few weeks since. Nick only heard about the conversations secondhand. This was the first time he'd talked to the man since saying his goodbyes.

"Sage is great." Dwight's tone reflected genuine happiness for a brief moment. "Things on the personal front are great. On the work front, though ... ."

Nick didn't know why Dwight was calling, but it was obvious that things had taken a serious turn. Dwight wouldn't call otherwise. He wouldn't put Maddie on the spot like that. Nick wasn't sure he cared how desperate Dwight was due to his current caseload ... and whatever else might be going on. He wouldn't risk Maddie regardless. "Well, I hope things go better for you at work."

Dwight knew he was being brushed off and refused to allow it. "I need to talk to Maddie. I called her phone twice, but she didn't answer."

"She's right here with me."

"I gathered that when you talked to her a few minutes ago," Dwight said dryly. "May I speak to her?"

Nick had a decision to make. Maddie sat cradled on his lap, her blue eyes wide and full of anger because he refused to hand over his phone. Dwight sounded uncomfortable on the other end, as if he were struggling with duty and loyalty, but resigned to following through no matter what.

"I don't know," Nick hedged, opting for honesty. "Something just happened and ... I'm afraid of what you want to talk to her about." He saw no reason to lie. "Maybe you and I should talk instead."

Nick could practically see Dwight's mind working on the other end of the call. "I can do that," Dwight said after a beat. "You're not going to be happy regardless, though. I promise you that."

"I've already figured that out myself." Nick flicked his eyes to Maddie. He could practically feel the anger emanating from her pores. "Tell me what you have and we'll go from there."

"I have twenty dead bodies and even more missing girls, although that number is shaky due to the sort of women we seem to be dealing with. It's not good."

"No. Start from the beginning."

That's exactly what Dwight did.

"YOU'RE NOT GOING."

Nick was firm as he watched Maddie pace her kitschy magic store an hour later, hands on her hips and flaxen hair flying. Maude wisely took a step back when she realized Maddie was merely overwhelmed by a vision rather than legitimately sick, but Nick had a feeling the elderly curmudgeon wasn't far away and would lodge her opinion if she felt it necessary.

"I am going." Maddie stopped moving long enough to fix Nick with a hard look. "You can't stop me from going."

Nick wasn't a fan of her tone. In general, they rarely argued. They were far too gooey and lost in each other for that. When it came to Maddie's safety, though, he had no problem putting his foot down. "Oh, that's where you're wrong, love."

"No, that's where *you're* wrong." Maddie spent years hiding from confrontation, refusing to assert herself because it simply wasn't her way. Since returning to Blackstone Bay – and more importantly Nick – she'd managed to find her stride. She was not the fearful teenager Nick bade goodbye to all those years before. She was still the Maddie he loved even then, but she was stronger now. He liked that about her ... except in instances like this when he felt she was putting her life on the line.

"Maddie, I'm not going to let you waltz off and put yourself in danger." It took all the resolve Nick had to keep his anger in check. "I told you what Dwight said."

"Yes, you told me what Dwight said," Maddie agreed. "You had a conversation with him that revolved around what he needed from me and completely cut me out of the decision making. I'm well aware of that."

Nick recognized the tone, knew he was in a precarious position, and yet pushed forward all the same. "Dwight is a cop."

"Really? I never would've guessed," Maddie drawled.

"The sarcasm isn't necessary."

"Please. I live with you and Granny. Apparently I'm the only one not allowed to engage in sarcasm, huh?"

Nick absolutely hated arguing with Maddie, but he loved her more than he disliked fighting. He would do whatever it took to keep her safe. That included engaging in a screaming match, which was something they'd yet to do despite their passionate relationship. They simply weren't fighters, and the few times they'd engaged in raised voices and hurt feelings, it gutted them both.

"Maddie, what do you want me to say?" Nick forced himself to remain reasonable. "What is it that you expect me to do here?"

"I want you to say that you understand."

"I do understand. I understand that Dwight called you and told you about missing girls and you want to help."

"No, Dwight told me more than that," Maddie countered. "Actually, Dwight told you more than that. In fact, he told you everything. I had to hear secondhand."

Nick ran his tongue over his teeth, conflicted. "And that upsets you, huh?"

"Oh, do you think?" Maddie rolled her eyes. "Why would it possibly upset me that you took a call that was meant for me and you told Dwight I wouldn't be coming to the city help him?"

"I'm starting to get the feeling that you believe I overstepped my bounds."

"Starting?"

"Maddie, you fainted."

"Stop saying that word!" Maddie's voice ratcheted up a notch. "I didn't faint. I ... saw something."

"And I really want to understand." Nick was plaintive. "Tell me what you saw, Mad."

"Do you care?" Maddie knew she was being belligerent, but she couldn't stop herself. "Does it matter what I saw? I think you've already made up your mind."

"Tell me," Nick prodded.

"I saw girls. I saw them running ... and crying ... and dying. I saw what Dwight told you about, the dark alley with the dead bodies. It was as if there was a field of them, all laid out on concrete and covered in garbage. I saw it all."

"Because Dwight called you?" Nick queried. "Did you see it because his call made it happen?"

"I don't know. Don't you dare blame Dwight, though."

"I have no intention of blaming Dwight," Nick argued. "That doesn't mean I want you hopping in your car and heading to Detroit either. It's not your job to solve that case, Mad."

Maddie had no idea exactly what Dwight told Nick. All she knew was that Nick related much of the conversation to her in measured tones, although she was certain he left out some of the gorier details. She knew what she saw in the vision, though, and she was certain she wouldn't be able to shake it whether she headed to Detroit to help Dwight or not. It would stick with her, haunt her, maybe even eat her alive. She didn't want that.

"He wouldn't have called if he didn't believe I could help, Nick," Maddie pressed.

Nick tamped down a twinge of distress because she didn't call him "Nicky." It wasn't exactly the end of the world, but it bothered him all the same. That was always her "go-to" term of endearment. "I'm sure he does believe you can help, Mad." He swallowed hard. "That doesn't mean you should help."

"Why not?"

"Because ... ." Nick broke off, unsure how to proceed.

"There were twenty dead girls in that alley, Nicky," Maddie noted. "There are more girls missing. They were stalked ... and hurt for a long time ... and then killed. There might be more out there waiting to get saved."

"And you might put yourself on a killer's radar if you try to help."

"I won't. I'll be helping Dwight. No one else will know."

"I'll know."

"They're dead girls, Nicky." Maddie refused to back down. "That could've been me. You know that, right?"

Nick rebelled at the thought. "Well, it wasn't you. You're here ... and you're safe. I want to keep you that way."

"And what if I want to help?"

"Maddie, you have a good heart and I know you always want to help, but this isn't your problem," Nick argued. "You don't live in the city. You live here. You can't go down there and fix multiple problems whenever Dwight has an issue. That's not fair to you."

"You're not arguing for me. You're arguing for you. You're the one who doesn't want me to go."

Nick's patience frayed. "Fine! I don't want you to go. I'm an ogre who doesn't want his girlfriend to put herself in danger. Start flogging me now."

Maddie refused to be dragged into a fight. "There are girls missing. They're probably being tortured, at least if what I saw in my head is true. I can't just forget about that. I can't just let it go."

Nick folded his arms over his chest, obstinate. "It's not your job to solve Dwight's case, Maddie. This isn't your concern."

"I'm going."

Nick inadvertently cringed. "You're not."

"I am."

"You're not."

"You're not the boss of me, Nicky," Maddie snapped, hating the sound of her voice as it cracked. "Dwight asked for my help. He wouldn't have called unless he was desperate. I know you recognize that."

"I hardly think it matters why he did it."

"It does to me. I'm going."

"You're not going, Maddie!" Nick lost his remaining restraint in an explosion of fiery temper and disbelief. "I won't just sit back and watch you put yourself at risk. No, don't look at me that way. It's not simply the physical risk I'm worried about. It's the emotional one, too. Look what happened today when you caught a glimpse of what's been going on down there. It's only going to get worse if you insert yourself in the middle of that investigation."

"It's because of that glimpse I can't turn away," Maddie countered. "I've seen what's happening. I can't look elsewhere. I can't forget. It's not in me. Besides ... I owe Dwight. He looked out for me when I lived down there. He did his very best to make sure I wasn't forgotten. He was the only one who did that."

The words were like a dagger in Nick's heart. He should've gone after her when she left. He always believed it and he couldn't help but wonder if his inaction was a catalyst for their current predicament. Nick took a steadying breath.

"I don't want to boss you around, Mad, but I'm at the point where I guess I'm going to have to be firm." Nick chose his words carefully. "You're not going. I won't let you put yourself at risk. I'm putting my foot down."

Maddie was inexplicably sad. "I'm going and you can't stop me. I'm an adult and my friend needs me. I'm going to help him. That's what you do when you care about someone. You help."

"Maddie ... ."

Maddie held up a hand to quiet him. "I'm going. There's nothing you can do to change my mind. I'm sorry if that upsets you, but I can't sit back and do nothing. I won't be able to live with myself if I don't try. So ... I'm sorry. I'll be leaving in the morning. If you can't accept that ... well, it's on you."

With those words, Maddie turned on her heel and left the room. Nick watched her go, anger coursing through him. He'd lost control of the situation and there was no going back. Only one question remained: Now what?

3. **THREE**

Maddie spent the evening sitting at her computer and reading news stories on the body find, hopping between news outlets in an attempt to get more information. She couldn't find the information she was looking for – everything was too fluid on the ground – but she did discover a few interesting tidbits and she couldn't tear her eyes from the reports.

One girl disappeared on her way home from the bar.

One woman was last seen near a bus stop on Woodward.

One woman was believed to have been taken from her home.

Another woman was believed to have gotten in a car with a john and was never seen again.

The information was sketchy and police were currently chasing leads and trying to put together a timeline. Maddie took advantage of Nick's ominous silence and called Dwight. He apologized profusely for causing problems, but Maddie waved off his concern and promised to text him as soon as she hit town the next day. It would be a long drive but there was no way she could ignore the issue now that she knew about it.

She packed while Nick was downstairs talking on the phone. He refused to look at her when she passed through the room and the guilt she felt was all-encompassing. That didn't mean she could turn back. Ultimately she ceded the bedroom they shared and headed downstairs to conduct research, and by the time she returned to the room Nick was already in bed staring at the ceiling.

Maddie paused by the door, her heart constricting. They hadn't been this far apart since they got together and her stomach was full of acid and fear when she edged into the room. "Do you want me to sleep somewhere else?"

Nick flicked his eyes to her, his expression unreadable. He hadn't spoken to her since the afternoon blowup. "Is that what you want?"

"No, but ... I don't want to upset you."

"I think it's too late for that, Maddie." Nick clasped his hands behind his head as he regarded her. "What have you been doing?"

It should've been an easy question to answer, but Maddie knew it would be the exact opposite.

"Researching news stories on the case," she replied after a beat. "They were all young women in their twenties. They disappeared in a variety of different ways. The stories don't say how the women were killed and Dwight didn't want to get into it over the phone."

"So ... you talked to him?"

Maddie pressed her lips together and nodded.

"And I see you've packed." Nick's eyes migrated to the suitcase by the door. "It's all set for you, huh? You're going to run off to face off with a serial killer and I have no say in it whatsoever."

Maddie's heart pinched. "Nicky."

"Don't." Nick shook his head, flashes of anger and helplessness whipping over his handsome features. "I don't want to start screaming at you so just ... don't."

Maddie reluctantly nodded. "I'm sorry. I can't just let it go though, Nicky. I won't be able to live with myself if I do."

"And what about me?" Nick challenged, his eyes on fire. "Do you think I'll be able to live with it if something happens to you?"

"No. Nothing will happen to me, though. Dwight won't let it."

Nick made a disgusted sound in the back of his throat. "That doesn't exactly make me feel better."

"I would say or do almost anything to make you feel better."

"Except call Dwight and tell him you're not going."

Maddie shook her head, firm. "No. I won't do that."

"Then I guess we're at an impasse."

"I guess we are."

The duo lapsed into uncomfortable silence, eyeing one another with wary worry. Finally, Maddie couldn't take another moment of it.

"Do you want me to sleep somewhere else?"

"No."

Nick's answer caught Maddie off guard. "You don't?"

"We're getting married, Maddie," Nick reminded her. "We're going to fight. That's what married couples do. That doesn't mean I want to be away from you ... especially since you're leaving tomorrow."

The relief that flooded through Maddie was almost enough to bring her to her knees. She undressed quickly, sliding into an old T-shirt before hitting the light and climbing into bed next to him. For a moment, she wondered if they would sleep in the same bed without touching. It was almost unbearable for her to fathom.

Then, as if he understood her conflicted thoughts, Nick slid his arm around her waist and tugged her so her head rested on his shoulder. He pressed a kiss to her forehead and rubbed his hand over her back.

"I love you," Maddie croaked out, her voice breaking. "I love you so much it hurts sometimes. I don't mean to hurt you. I just can't ignore what I saw."

"I know." Nick's voice was barely a whisper. "I love you, too. Nothing will ever change that. Not even you being a stubborn mule."

Maddie chuckled as she sniffled. "I think you're a stubborn mule, too."

"Yeah, we're quite the pair." Nick let loose with a loud sigh as he snuggled Maddie closer. "Get some sleep, love. You're going to have a full day ahead of you tomorrow."

"Okay." Maddie rested her hand on the spot above Nick's heart. "I think I'm going to see a few things in my dreams tonight. I apologize ahead of time if I wake you."

"Don't ever apologize for that, Mad. We're together – for better or worse – and I want to be here when you need me. That's my job."

"You're good at your job."

"We both are." Nick pressed a soft kiss to the corner of her mouth. "Sleep, Mad. I'll be right here if you need me."

"You always are."

MADDIE DIDN'T SLEEP WELL. She didn't expect to, of course, but the visions chased her throughout the night, never giving her an hour at a time of uninterrupted sleep, and she woke more tired than when she went to bed.

Nick was in the kitchen when she dragged her suitcase downstairs. He was up before her, although she had no idea what he did in the early morning hours before dawn, and he stood at the stove cooking breakfast when she popped into the kitchen.

"You look rough," Maude noted as she drank her coffee at the table.

"Thank you, Granny." Maddie didn't bother hiding her eye roll. "I feel a bit rough."

Nick studied her for a long beat. "You didn't sleep much. I felt you shifting."

"I'm sorry."

"We've been over this, Mad. Don't apologize for things you can't control. I don't blame you for waking me. I'm upset because I couldn't soothe you."

Maddie balked. "You soothe me just by breathing."

Nick's expression softened, although only marginally. "Right back at you, love."

"Oh, geez." Maude rubbed her forehead, clearly disturbed. "Even when you fight you're sickly sweet."

Nick managed a weak grin. "I'm glad we can remain predictable even when times get rough." He turned his full attention to the stove. "I'm cooking hash browns and eggs, Mad. Do you want toast, too?"

In truth, Maddie's stomach wasn't keen on the idea of food. Since

Nick was going out of his way to offer her an olive branch before she left, though, there was no way she could turn her back on it or him. "I'll make the toast."

"Okay."

Maddie shuffled around the edge of the counter, stopping next to Nick long enough to roll to the balls of her feet and press a kiss to his cheek. He turned to her, his lips curving as he noted the myriad of emotions flitting through her eyes.

"I love you," Nick whispered, brushing his lips against her mouth. "It's okay."

Maddie wasn't sure that was true, but she appreciated the effort. "I love you more."

"I don't think that's possible."

"I guess we'll just have to agree to disagree."

"I guess so."

Maddie gave him another quick kiss before retrieving the bread from the counter. She took a moment to collect herself and then focused on Maude. "You need to be good while I'm gone. If you get in trouble, I won't be here to bail you out of jail."

"I'm pretty sure that was an insult," Maude said dryly. "Do you really think I'm dumb enough to get caught by the cops? The cops in this town are idiots ... no offense, Nick."

Nick rolled his eyes. "Why would I possibly take offense at that?"

"Who knows." Maude airily waved off the question. "You guys are so sensitive I can't keep up with your fragile feelings from moment to moment. You have nothing to worry about, though. I promise I'll be fine while you guys are out of town."

"I hope that's a promise you'll be able to keep," Maddie said pointedly. "In fact ... wait." She wrinkled her nose as she ran Maude's words through her busy brain. "Nick will be here to keep you in line. You need to do what he says while I'm gone."

Maude snorted derisively. "Nick isn't going to be around. He's going with you. In fact, I'm thinking about having a party while the two of you are out of town."

"Nick isn't going with me. He has work." Maddie shifted her eyes to Nick and found him watching her with unreadable eyes. "Right?"

"I considered waiting for you to ask me to go with you, but then I realized you weren't going to do it," he said quietly. "I was hurt by that, thinking you didn't want me with you."

"That's not true," Maddie protested, horrified. "I didn't want to ask because I knew you would go and that didn't seem like a fair position to put you in."

"So you think it's better to leave me here to worry?" Nick challenged.

"I ... ." Maddie broke off and chewed her bottom lip.

"Yeah, I can see you didn't even consider it because you thought you were doing the right thing for me," Nick said. "That makes me feel a little better, although I'm not going to lie, I'm still agitated."

Maddie worked overtime to keep the tears burning the back of her eyes from falling. "But ... you're going with me?"

Nick took pity on her and grabbed her hand. "I wouldn't let you do something like this without me. You should know that."

Maddie wanted to remain strong. She was desperate for it. She opened her mouth to offer him a firm and stern "thank you" without engaging in any sort of drama. Instead she burst into tears and threw her arms around his neck. "Oh, thank you so much."

Nick's stomach twisted when he realized exactly how worked up she'd been. "Don't thank me, love." He tightened his arms around her. "We're a unit. For better or for worse, it's you and me together for the rest of our lives. If one of us is going on an adventure, you'd better understand that both of us are going on an adventure."

"You have no idea how relieved I am." Maddie pulled back so she could swipe at her falling tears. "I wasn't sure I could do this without you, but I was afraid to ask. What are you going to do about work?"

"I called Dale," Nick replied, referring to his partner. "He said I could take some vacation time since things have been slow. He didn't have a problem with it."

"But ... do you have a problem with it?"

"I have a much bigger problem being separated from you."

"Me, too." Maddie's arms were back around Nick's neck. "I love you so much. I ... thank you. Just ... thank you."

"Maddie, I love you. Nothing will ever keep us apart. I promise. No matter how angry I am – and make no mistake, I'm not thrilled how this shook out – I will always be with you if given the option. Never doubt that."

"I promise to remember that." Maddie was solemn. "I'll do better."

"You're already perfect." Nick graced her with a soft kiss as he worked overtime to ignore the gagging noises Maude made as she mimed throwing up. "Everything is going to be okay. I promise."

MADDIE SAID HER GOODBYES to Maude, making sure to call her best friend Christy Ford and request the occasional drop-in to make sure Maude didn't lose control of her faculties ... or turn the house into party central. It was almost eight before Maddie and Nick hit the road and Nick was relieved to find that Maddie seemed much more relaxed than when she had first joined him in the kitchen.

"Let's talk about what you saw in your vision," Nick prodded as he pointed his truck toward the freeway. "I want to be as current as possible on the case before we hit Detroit."

"I don't know what more to tell you," Maddie hedged. "I basically saw glimpses of various girls running away ... or cowering. I saw a few being ... um ... attacked."

Nick kept his eyes on the road but linked his fingers with Maddie's to offer her comfort. "How were they attacked?"

"He had a knife. I saw a lot of ... blood. I think he toys with them before he kills them, though."

"Toys how?"

"He makes it into a game when he stalks them." Maddie rolled her neck as she stared out the passenger window. "He tries to isolate them so it doesn't matter how loud they scream."

"That's a gutsy move," Nick noted. "How does he know he can stalk them in a city and not get caught? I mean ... I can see something like that happening in the country. We have so much open space in Blackstone Bay that it could easily happen in our neck of the woods. A city is different, though."

"It's Detroit," Maddie pointed out.

"Still."

"How much time have you spent there?"

The question caught Nick off guard. "I honestly haven't spent more than a few days here and there. When I was in the academy, we drove to the city and spent a week attending classes at one of the facilities at Wayne State University. I didn't think that area was so bad."

"That's because it's not bad. That's a revered school and the security is tight. The city itself is ... different."

Nick didn't miss the shift in her tone. "Different how?"

"Well, for starters, it's not all rundown buildings and gangbangers," Maddie replied. "There's definitely violence, drugs, prostitution, and muggers, so be careful. I'll be leaving my purse in the hotel and traveling with money in my pockets once we arrive."

"I'll take care of the money. You just make sure to stay close to me."

"We'll fight about money when we land," Maddie said. "There's no way you're paying for all of this. It's my deal so I should be the one to foot the bill."

"We're getting married. Your money is my money and vice versa."

"You have a point."

"I'm the smartest man in the world and you should always listen to what I say," Nick teased, squeezing her hand. "Go back to what you were saying about the city, though."

"Oh, right." Maddie shook her head to dislodge money thoughts. They would discuss that later, and hopefully they wouldn't get into another fight. "The city is really hard to explain. Some pockets are wonderful and full of culture. Those areas are clean and very little violence occurs.

"A lot of the neighborhoods are abandoned, though," she continued. "Detroit's population continues to plummet despite efforts to entice people into the city. What happens in those neighborhoods is that homes are abandoned or seized by the bank and then used as drug houses ... or sometimes worse. No one can keep up on patrolling the abandoned houses in every neighborhood."

Nick arched an eyebrow, legitimately curious. "What's worse?"

"There's a big drug trafficking problem in Detroit because of the city's proximity to the border."

"Oh." Nick rolled his neck. "I guess that makes sense. I never really thought about it."

"A lot of people go missing in Detroit, too," Maddie explained. "Because of the nature of the city, though, it's difficult to tell if people voluntarily go missing or something else happened. It makes Dwight's job extremely difficult.

"In this case, though, they know that they have a predator on the loose," she continued. "This is something tangible that Dwight can solve."

"And you want to help."

"I *need* to help," Maddie corrected. "Now that I've seen them, witnessed what they've gone through, I can't simply turn my back and walk away. I need to do what I can to help."

"I understand that, Mad." Nick's tone was gentle. "You can't bring back the ones already lost, though."

"No," Maddie agreed. "I can't do that. I can talk to the spirits left behind if they're still hanging around. I can maybe get a sense of the killer and relate that news to Dwight. He wouldn't put me in danger for anything. Just because I won't be on the front lines, though, that doesn't mean I can't help."

Nick gave her a measuring look. "I guess I didn't think of that. I'm sorry for demanding you see things my way, although I'm still leery. However, we need to come to an agreement before we land."

Maddie was instantly on alert. "And what agreement is that?"

"We stick together," Nick answered without hesitation. "I won't get in the way of you helping, but you need to agree to keep me close so I don't spend the next few days freaking out. I don't think that's too much to ask."

"So you want a compromise." Maddie rubbed her chin as she considered the suggestion. "I think that's fair," she said after a beat. "We'll do this together. We are a unit, after all."

"Now and forever." Nick lifted their joined hands and kissed the back of her knuckles. "Just for the record, this was an easy compromise to make. I have a feeling the rest won't be so easy. Even when we fight, Mad, I need you to know that I love you."

Maddie's smile was small but heartfelt. "I feel the same way. It's going to be a stressful few days, but I know we can make it through."

"We'll definitely make it through this. There's no other option for me besides you."

"Right back at you."

"Good." Nick sucked in a calming breath. "Now, tell me about the locations you saw in the vision. I want to know everything you can tell me. When we hit the city, we'll talk to Dwight and go from there."

"That sounds like a plan."

4. FOUR

Maddie knew where Dwight's precinct was located, so after they dropped off their luggage at the hotel – Nick insisted on an upgrade once they were on their way – the couple pointed themselves in Dwight's direction.

Nick, who had never spent a lot of time in the city, kept his arm around Maddie's back as they walked down the sidewalk. For her part, Maddie couldn't stop smiling as she enjoyed the way he scanned the crowd.

"I never thought I would be the brave one."

It took Nick a moment to realize Maddie was speaking. "What?" He flicked his eyes to her. "Did you say something?"

Maddie's giggle was enough to warm Nick's heart even though he was on edge.

"I never thought I would be the brave one," Maddie repeated. "I'm more familiar with the city than you and I can tell you're nervous."

Most men would've felt ridiculous about being called out on such behavior, but Nick wasn't most men. "I can't believe you lived here," he admitted, shifting his eyes to two women across the street. They were very clearly prostitutes, soliciting any man who passed, and their overt actions made him uncomfortable. "I used to picture it."

"Picture what?"

"The city. Well, to get technical, I used to picture you in the city. After you left me, I mean."

Maddie pressed her lips together. Their separation remained a sore spot between them even though they'd talked everything out. "I'm sorry, Nicky. I wish I could take it back. I ... ."

"Shh." Nick shook his head. "I didn't mean to make you feel guilty. That's not what I was saying. It's just ... whenever I pictured you it was in a park or smiling at some guy, which made me incredibly jealous at the thought. I had no idea who the guy was, mind you, but I always imagined you were off somewhere being happy."

"That wasn't possible without you."

Nick's grin was genuine. "Yeah, I think we were both miserable."

Maddie offered up an impish smile. "Devastated."

"Crushed."

"Annihilated."

"Forever haunted."

Nick planted a swift kiss on her mouth. "We're safe from all that now, though."

"Definitely."

The couple jolted at the sound of a slow clap, turning slowly to find Dwight leaning against the wall of his precinct as he eyed them with obvious amusement. "Oh, that was so cute. I see you guys are just as annoying as you were when I saw you last."

"More so." Nick sobered and extended his hand. "It's nice to see you."

Dwight snagged Nick's serious gaze with a sober one of his own. "Thanks for trying to say that even though I know you don't mean it."

"I mean it," Nick argued. "I'm happy to see you. I simply wish it was under different circumstances."

"We all wish that." Dwight turned his full attention to Maddie, and even though it was a serious moment, he couldn't stop himself from smiling. "You look all shiny and happy."

Maddie slid away from Nick so she could give Dwight a heartfelt hug. "I don't know about the shiny part, but I'm definitely happy."

"Oh, you're shiny." Dwight rested his hand on her shoulder. "You two seem happy, other than the fact that I dragged you away from home and caused a fight, that is."

"How do you know you caused a fight?" Nick asked.

Dwight shrugged. "Maddie and I talked a bit last night. She didn't come right out and say it, but I could tell she was unhappy. I'm glad you appear to have made up."

"It's not that I don't want her to help you," Nick hedged. "It's simply that I don't want her in danger. That's why I put up a fight."

"Do you think I want to put her in danger?"

"No, but that doesn't necessarily mean anything," Nick replied. "She always tends to find trouble. She can't help herself. I don't want her finding trouble down here ... and especially with this case. You have a bunch of dead women. I don't want Maddie to join them."

"We won't let Maddie join them." Dwight was firm. "As for the women, I was just coming back from the medical examiner's office with the preliminary autopsy reports to go over. It looks as if we have twenty of them, which was my original guess."

"Twenty women?" Maddie was horrified even though she'd heard the number before. It was somehow sobering to have it confirmed. "You're sure about that?"

"I'm sure. We don't have complete bodies for some of them but ... we're pretty sure."

Nick tilted his head to the side. "What do you mean about not having full bodies?"

"We have ten bodies that are mostly intact," Dwight replied. "That's not all of them by a long shot, but we have ten that are complete other than some scavenger damage. The rest are ... um, pieces ... of women."

Maddie clutched Nick's hand tighter as he slid his free arm around her back and tugged her to his chest. "That's awful."

"It is," Dwight agreed. "We had no idea this was going on and now we're in quite the pickle. We have twenty dead women. Another fifteen to thirty who could be missing. We have a predator on the loose and exactly no leads."

"And that's why you want me, right?" Maddie asked.

Dwight nodded. "I don't want to put you in danger, Maddie. I agree with Nick on that one. If you could find one of the girl's ghosts, though, you might be able to get answers and point us in the right direction. That's all I'm going to ask of you."

"Okay. Where do you want to start?" Maddie was gung-ho so she didn't initially notice the two detectives walking past their small group. She also didn't notice the odd looks they cast in her direction.

Nick noticed, though. He was the observant sort. At first he thought the detectives were interested in Maddie for her looks. She was frustratingly unaware of her appeal and didn't so much as glance in their direction. After several moments of quiet study, though, Nick realized something else was going on ... and the emotions swamping him weren't of the comfortable variety.

"We should take this someplace else," Dwight said after a beat, his eyes trained on the detectives. "Do you guys need something?" he asked them pointedly.

"We were just checking out your friend, Dwight," the nearest detective replied, holding Nick's challenging gaze for a moment before continuing. "I thought I might've recognized her and wanted to get a better look."

Maddie snapped her eyes in the man's direction, frowning when she recognized him. "Detective Strawser, you don't have to play dumb. We both know you remember me."

"I do indeed, Ms. Graves," Strawser drawled with a lazy grin. "I mean ... who could forget you?"

"No one with eyes," the other detective supplied.

"That will be enough of that," Dwight barked. "Ms. Graves is here by my invitation. If you don't like that, Strawser, you can take it up with the chief. He's the one who okayed her consulting."

"Consulting?" Strawser let loose with a derisive snort. "Is that what we're calling it now?"

"What would you call it?" Nick challenged, keeping a firm grip on Maddie.

"I would call it nonsense," Strawser replied without hesitation.

"Not everyone here believes that woman's psychic song and dance routine."

"I said that was enough," Dwight hissed. "I don't care what you want. This isn't your case, so mind your own business."

"Fine. I didn't mean to stir up trouble." Strawser held up his hands in a placating manner. "I honestly apologize, Ms. Graves. I hope the spirits aren't unhappy with you so you can help find the fiend committing these atrocities."

Strawser said the words, but the sparkle in his eyes indicated he didn't mean them.

"I hope so, too," Maddie said lightly. "It was nice to see you again, Detective Strawser."

"Charmed, I'm sure," Strawser said, lowering his voice so only his cohort could hear as they made their way up the steps that led to the precinct's main entrance. The duo burst into an uncomfortable fit of laughter before disappearing inside.

Dwight watched Maddie with interest, waiting long enough that Strawser was long out of hearing distance before continuing. "Why don't we head to Mexicantown for lunch, huh? I have some things to talk to you about."

Nick nodded, his shoulders stiff. "Fine. Lead the way."

"Mexican sounds good." Maddie found her voice and was happy it didn't crack as she regrouped. "I haven't had good Mexican in more than a year. Let's go to our favorite restaurant."

Dwight bobbed his head. "It's as if you're reading my mind."

NICK WAS HAPPY TO cuddle close with Maddie as they settled in one side of a cozy booth. Since he was unfamiliar with the various areas of Detroit – the bulk of his knowledge coming from television shows and news reports – he was pleasantly surprised when he saw the restaurant Dwight selected for them.

After placing orders and accepting their drinks, talk turned to the murders and Dwight didn't bother to hide his unease.

"I'm sorry that you got caught up in all of this again right out of the gate, Maddie," he offered, his expression contrite. "I was hoping they wouldn't see you – at least not yet – and that's why I was waiting outside."

Nick ran his tongue over his teeth as he debated what to say, keeping his eyes on Maddie as she squirmed beside him.

"You don't have to be sorry," Maddie said after a moment's quiet contemplation. "You didn't create the situation, Dwight. You took as much abuse as I did back then. I'm sure you didn't want to call me for that reason alone."

"I wanted to see you," Dwight stressed. "I was hoping to come north this summer and spend some time in Blackstone Bay, bring the wife and make it a proper vacation. Sage is looking forward to seeing you again, too. She's home for spring break. This was not how I wanted to see you again."

"And yet here we are." Maddie held her hands palms out and shrugged. "We can't go back in time and undo what was done. We can only move forward. It might be uncomfortable for both of us, but if we can come up with the necessary answers – if we can save some lives – then I would say it was well worth it."

Dwight opened his mouth but shut it before commenting. Ultimately he merely shrugged and smiled.

"You got your way two days in a row, Mad," Nick teased, poking her side. "This being forceful thing is really working out for you, huh?"

Maddie beamed, the expression lighting up her beautiful face. "It really is. I should've been forceful a long time ago."

"I like you however you are." Nick patted the top of her hand. "In fact, I'm pretty sure I like you best when you're with me and smiling."

"Ha, ha." Maddie nudged Nick out of the way so she could scoot off the booth seat. "I'll be right back. I need to run to the restroom."

Nick nodded as he watched her go, keeping his gaze level until she disappeared through the door and then his expression shifted. "We don't have a lot of time, so why don't you just tell me what's going on and we'll try to figure out how to handle it before she gets back."

Dwight's eyebrows flew up his forehead. "You want to discuss Maddie's involvement in my case without her?"

"Oh, don't give me that." Nick rolled his neck. "I want her safe. I'm not going to apologize for that. I know you're aware that we got in a huge fight about this last night, so don't bother pretending otherwise."

"You obviously made up."

"We did make up," Nick agreed. "We made up because I gave in. She was coming down here to help you no matter what – because she feels she owes you – and I could either get with the program or sit at home and pout. As unhappy as I am with the situation, there was no way I could allow her to come down here alone and put herself at risk simply because I was upset. That's not how I roll."

Dwight absently played with the ring of condensation his glass left on the table. "Do you honestly think I would purposely put her in a position where she could get hurt? Is that what you think I want for her?"

"No." Nick didn't hesitate when shaking his head. "I think you care about her a great deal."

"But ... ?"

"But I think you're desperate to solve this case and you can't see straight where she's concerned," Nick answered, unruffled. "I'm not going to pretend that I'm happy with your decision, but I honestly do get it. I'm a cop, too. I don't see the things you see, but I want justice as much as the next person when it comes to what you found in that alley.

"The thing is, you want to use the person I love most in this world as a weapon of sorts," he continued. "I know how this is going to work. You're going to drag her to the alley and watch her perform like an elephant at the circus. You don't think that puts her in danger, but I'm worried you're wrong."

"How is that going to put her in danger?" Dwight pressed. "I mean, I get that you're territorial where she's concerned. You two went through hell to find your way back to one another. You love each other to distraction. How is taking her to the scene going to put her in danger, though? I want to know, because I spent hours stressing over the call to make sure there was no way that could possibly happen and now you're saying it will most likely happen."

"I'm not saying it will most likely happen," Nick corrected hastily. "I said it was a possibility. I have no idea what this alley looks like, but I'm guessing the neighborhood has regular visitors and that perhaps the killer is someone familiar to everyone down there.

"What's going to happen when you take a blond who looks like Maddie to a bad neighborhood and let her loose to walk around and talk to ghosts?" he continued. "She's going to draw a crowd. And, if the killer is local, he might be hanging around the area in an effort to keep his ear to the ground and figure out exactly how much you guys know."

Dwight steepled his fingers and rested his elbows on the table. "I considered that. Even if the killer sees her with us, though, he's not going to make a move on her. Maddie will be in and out of the city before he has a chance to figure out who she is. She won't be in danger. I won't let her be in danger."

Nick heaved out a sigh. "I'll die for her, and willingly so, but that doesn't mean I think she's completely free of danger here. Why do you think I insisted on coming?"

Dwight arched an eyebrow. "Honestly? I figured you knew your limitations and realized you couldn't be away from her for twenty-four hours let alone a few days. If you let her storm off, you would've followed by tomorrow morning and we both know it. I thought you were simply acknowledging that fact."

Nick made a face. "I think you're saying I'm whipped."

"So, we both know you're whipped." Dwight's grin was cheeky. "It's okay. I kind of like that you dote on Maddie like you do. She was an unhappy woman when I knew her and she almost broke my heart. You've fixed all of that."

"I'm doing my best."

"And you're worried that I'm trying to take all of that from you," Dwight added, waving his hand when Nick opened his mouth to argue. "I know you don't think I'm doing it on purpose, but I honestly can't stop myself from asking for help with this particular case.

"You weren't there, Nick," he continued, lowering his voice. "You didn't see those girls discarded like heaps of trash. Some of them were as young as my daughter. Some were as old as Maddie. How would you feel if Maddie was one of the women found in that alley?"

Nick balked. "That's what I'm trying to make sure doesn't happen."

"And I get that. You're her champion and you want to protect her. I would die for her, too, whether you believe that or not. I want to make sure that no one else dies, too, though. I want her to be safe and sound, but I also want to make sure that no other parents lose their child to a monster. I can't simply forget what I saw."

"I'm not asking you to." Nick knew he'd already lost the argument. He understood Dwight's plight and even though he wanted Maddie away from danger, dragging her off and putting her under lock and key wasn't an option. "Ultimately it doesn't matter anyway. Maddie is determined to see this through because that's who she is. It's my job to keep her safe."

"It's *our* job to keep her safe," Dwight corrected. "I think that together we'll be able to pull it off."

"I certainly hope so, because I can't lose her. I'm going to be on her like sequins on a Kardashian."

Dwight blinked several times in rapid succession, his face blank. "That's a really odd reference."

"Maude used it the other day and it sort of stuck in my head." Nick was rueful. "It kind of ruins my street cred to talk about the Kardashians, doesn't it?"

"You have no idea. It will be our little secret, though."

"I appreciate that."

5. FIVE

The alley was close enough to walk to after lunch. Since it was early spring, the air turned brisk and Nick was glad he remembered to bring a coat. He made sure to keep Maddie between him and Dwight during the walk, and the conversation was heavy as they navigated the rundown area.

"The thing is, we knew a lot of the women were missing before the bodies were discovered," Dwight explained. "It's hard in this area, though, because a lot of the women are either working girls or high-risk victims."

"What does 'high risk' mean?" Maddie asked.

"He means that they're involved in a bevy of high risk activities," Nick replied. "It could be drugs or simply hanging around with the wrong crowd." He scanned the buildings as they passed, doing his best not to make a face at the broken windows and filthy landings. "This is a rough area, so when someone goes missing the cops don't always assume it was due to murder or kidnapping."

"Oh." Maddie nodded, understanding dawning. "So low-risk victims would be more likely to come from the suburbs and stay away from drugs and booze."

"In essence," Dwight confirmed. "Even though several of the victims we've been able to identify so far were high risk, there were a few I wouldn't consider high risk. Tessa Roth, for example, worked as a nurse at the hospital and lived in an apartment about five blocks over. Her neighborhood wasn't so bad. There were a few others who had no ties to anything remotely high risk either."

"Did you think she took off, too? Tessa Roth, I mean," Nick asked.

"I've only been through the initial report on her disappearance. Her mother reported her missing after she went two weeks without a call. Tessa has been doing heavy rotations so she'd been very busy and her mother lives in Chicago. It was unheard of for them to go two weeks without speaking, but her mother noticed she wasn't checking in online and that's what tipped her off."

"What did you find when you searched her apartment?"

"I wasn't there, but the report said nothing seemed out of the ordinary," Dwight replied. "Tessa's purse was missing, but her phone was on the table. To me that suggests she ran out for a quick errand and never returned, but we didn't have enough evidence – or a motive, for that matter – to assume it was anything else at the time. Until we found her body, she was simply a missing person."

"And all the victims died the same way?" Nick pressed.

"Basically," Dwight replied, casting a furtive look in Maddie's direction. "They died hard."

"I already know how they died," Maddie noted, making sure not to meet Dwight's alarmed gaze. "I saw it in my head when you called."

"Yeah, about that ... ."

Maddie ignored the implied question. "I saw things that I wish I hadn't, but I didn't see the killer's face. I know that would help you, but I always saw him in shadow."

"And yet you're certain it's a man, right?"

"I am." Maddie bobbed her head. "Broad shoulders. Small waist. Long legs."

"What about height?" Dwight asked. "Can you give me a guess on that?"

"I ... hmm." Maddie pursed her lips as she considered the question. "I honestly don't know. I need to look at photos of the women you found – real ones, not the body ones – so I can put names with the faces I saw in my visions. That way we can look at their height and go from there."

"I'm sure we can make that happen." Dwight gestured toward a fenced-off parcel to their right. "This is it."

"This is it?" Nick pressed his hand to Maddie's lower back so he could maintain contact but turned his head in a variety of different directions as he searched the empty lot. It was marked off with police tape, but Dwight lifted it so they could walk on the property.

"This wasn't what I expected," Maddie admitted, taking a hesitant step forward. "This isn't what I saw."

Dwight and Nick exchanged uneasy looks. Maddie's voice had taken on a far-off quality that made both men nervous.

"What did you see, love?" Nick's voice was gentle as he rested his hand on her elbow. "Go slow. Just ... tell us what you saw."

"I saw the most with a blond woman," Maddie volunteered. "She seemed tall like me. Slim. Blue eyes that were full of fear."

Nick bit back his irritation at hearing Maddie describe a woman who sounded an awful lot like the one directly in front of him. "What else, Mad?"

"They were on what looked to be a sidewalk, but it was more like a narrow street," Maddie answered. "The woman wore a scarf. It was one of those knit ones, multiple colors, and it streamed after her. She knew she was in trouble, but she wore these ankle boot things that made it difficult to run because the sidewalks were icy."

Dwight perked up. "That means you saw something from the winter. That might help us narrow down who we're looking for."

"I don't know that it was winter," Maddie cautioned. "I didn't see snow. I only saw ice, although now that you mention it, there was a lot of ice ... almost as if it were a bad dream rather than reality."

Dwight rubbed his chin as he regarded her. "That could be from right after the ice storm we had."

"When was that?" Nick asked.

"Late February. The weather forecasters couldn't decide if we were going to get an ice storm or blizzard – you know how they waffle back and forth and know nothing – but we got the ice storm south of I-94 and a blizzard north. That has to be what you're talking about.

"The ice storm created quite a mess," he continued. "We were actually worse off than those who got all the snow because it weighed down the power lines and the roads were like a skating rink. I think we had something like three hundred and fifty accidents in Detroit alone in a twelve-hour period."

"Wow." Nick rubbed the back of his neck. "Still, that makes sense. No one without a specific agenda was out in an ice storm so our guy could hunt at his leisure."

"And Maddie said the woman wore high-heeled boots, which would've slowed her down," Dwight added. "You think it was an alley, though, that you saw her running through, right? Did you see any business names?"

Maddie licked her lips and thought hard. "I honestly didn't. I saw a big red trash receptacle, but that could belong to any business. I saw some steam from an open door, although it was only cracked. I got the distinct impression that it was a restaurant, but what kind is beyond me."

"That's okay." Dwight cracked a smile. "That's good. It's a start, at least."

"It's not as much as I hoped." Maddie took a step away from Nick and surveyed the lot. "This isn't technically an alley. It's an empty lot."

"It has alley access over there." Dwight pointed toward the back of the adjacent building. "This is an empty apartment complex. It hasn't been inhabited for two years and the floors are giving way in some spots. Quite a few people squat here to get out of the cold, but we went through it yesterday and we don't believe any of the victims were killed inside."

"How do you know that?" Maddie queried.

"No blood, love," Nick replied.

"Oh." Maddie rubbed her hands together. "I guess I should've figured that out myself." She was so intent on searching the lot she didn't bother looking in Nick's direction. He was thankful for that because he couldn't disguise his worry. "This isn't the place I saw, though. It's ... different."

"That doesn't surprise me," Dwight supplied. "We're pretty sure he only used this spot as dumping grounds."

"But ... why?" Maddie asked plaintively. "Why did he pick this spot? Do you know?"

"We can only theorize so far," Dwight answered. "I know you see ugliness when you look at this place, but it's honestly an intriguing location when you look at it from a law enforcement perspective."

"Tell me how," Maddie prodded, scuffing her feet against the ground as she moved forward.

Nick fought his instincts and let her move about freely. The lot was fenced off and she was in little danger from the outside world. He figured it was best to let her do what she wanted on her own timetable ... at least for now.

"It has easy access to roads." Dwight gestured to the east and south. "That way leads to the freeway. It's less than a block. This way has you on Gratiot in two turns. That road is busy, lots of traffic even in the middle of the night, and it's easy to disappear."

"What about the police presence down here?" Nick asked. "Your precinct is only a few blocks away."

"It is, but it's a big area. I would say we patrol this small corner once an hour, but if you know where to watch ... ."

"Then it's easy to avoid being caught," Nick finished. "Plus, if the guy is smart – which I think he would have to be to get away with this for so long – then he would know to come between two and five in the morning. That's when the shifts are smallest in every department. Heck, in Blackstone Bay we don't have anyone on the roads at that time."

"Blackstone Bay is a world all its own," Dwight said. "You're right, though. We only have two units on during those hours and if they pass this lot once during that time I would be surprised. Most of our issues come from the casinos during those hours."

"And where are the casinos in proximity to this spot?"

"About fifteen blocks that way," Dwight answered, pointing. "Not far but not really close. That late, the bulk of the trouble we have is from drunks leaving the casino and thieves watching to see who they can steal from."

"That makes sense." Nick turned so he could study the direction from which they entered the lot. A group of people – clearly interested in what was going on across the way – grouped together to watch the action. "I'm assuming you have normal snitches down here."

"We do," Dwight confirmed. "The thing is, our snitches turn on each other for drugs and prostitution. Occasionally you'll get a gang murder out here, but they keep those mostly to the abandoned neighborhoods several blocks out. This area is well and truly dead.

"People coming down to Mexicantown for the food park in the lots over there," he continued. "They don't come here."

"So the only people who come here are the ones who live here," Nick mused, shifting his eyes to the apartment complex two buildings down. He could see people moving in the windows. "I'm guessing that the people who live here don't have a lot of money."

"No, and the drug trade in this particular area isn't very big when compared to other areas," Dwight explained. "The people here can't afford it, although I think there was a gang shooting on this spot about six months ago if I remember correctly. The details aren't stuck in my head, but it was a big deal because it was the first shooting on this stretch in almost a year."

"It was a little girl," Maddie volunteered, causing Nick to snap his head in her direction. She'd traveled a good thirty feet while he'd been discussing the logistics of the neighborhood with Dwight and she was crouched down and staring at a large bush.

"Mad, what are you doing?" Nick moved to start in her direction, but Maddie held up her hand to stop him.

"Don't. You'll frighten her away."

"Her?" Dwight turned slowly, deliberately, and focused on Maddie. "Are you talking to a ... person? Is it one of our victims?"

Maddie swallowed hard as she stared at the ethereal child in front of her. The girl's brown eyes were large and luminous and the jeans she wore were clean and only frayed at the hems, as if someone – probably her mother – had let them out to get more use out of them.

"I'm talking to a victim," Maddie replied. "It's not one of the victims you're looking for, though."

"Oh." Dwight was at a loss and he looked to Nick for guidance.

Since Nick was still relatively new to the ghost game – although he was learning more each and every day – he wasn't sure how to answer. All he could do was shrug and hold out his hands.

"Her name is Tina Wydell," Maddie said, offering up a benign smile for the little girl only she could see. "She was crossing the street six months ago when shots rang out and she was killed."

Dwight pulled his phone from his pocket and typed something, staring hard at the small screen for several beats before lifting his chin. "You're right. She lived in the complex right across the way. According to the report, her mother said she was running to the corner store for milk and never returned home."

"What corner store?" Nick asked, glancing around.

"The liquor store," Dwight replied. "Most of these neighborhoods don't have markets because no one can make a profit with them thanks to the violence and theft. People in this area have to travel if they want groceries so a lot of the liquor stores carry a few staples."

Nick never yearned to live in the city and that inclination hadn't changed since landing in Detroit. "That's inexplicably sad."

"Welcome to the big city." Dwight forced a smile. "Is Tina the only ghost in this area, Maddie?"

"She is." Maddie mimed as if she was smoothing a child's hair and the heartbroken expression on her face was enough to tug at Nick's heartstrings. It was clear she was struggling with whatever she saw and he had no way to help her. "She's been hanging out here since she died because she occasionally gets to see her mother. That's all she lives for now."

"Why not go home?" Dwight asked. "Her apartment is less than a block away."

Maddie leaned her head to the side and listened for a minute, nodding in understanding at several points before licking her lips.

"Because Tina wasn't killed by some random person," she answered after collecting her thoughts. "She was killed by her brother. He fell in with the wrong crowd and was aiming for someone else, but Tina was in the way. By the time he saw her ... ."

"It was too late," Dwight finished, glancing back at his phone screen. "No one has ever been arrested for her death. I guess I can call in a tip to the gang task force and have them put some pressure on the brother."

Maddie turned her full attention to the little girl. "Do you want that? Do you want your brother to pay?"

Nick wished he could hear the conversation, but to him it was as if Maddie was talking to thin air. Occasionally he could hear Olivia, Maddie's mother, when she dropped in for a visit but more often than not those instances accompanied a distinct threat against Maddie. Those were the times Olivia could more easily gather her limited power and try to help her only daughter. Whatever was happening with Maddie now, Nick wasn't privy to the information so he could do nothing but watch.

"She doesn't want you to do that," Maddie said finally. "She has no love for her brother – who she says lied to police about where he was and what he was doing the day she died – but she doesn't want her mother to be alone. She doesn't think it would be fair."

Dwight wasn't sure he agreed, but he opted to let it go. "Can you ask her if she's seen anyone hanging out in this area? If she's really been here for six months, she might've seen our killer."

"Sure." Maddie lowered her voice and whispered to the girl, allowing Dwight and Nick to have a moment.

"I hate this part of what she can do," Nick muttered, restlessly combing a hand through his dark hair. "It's so hard on her. She's got such a big heart and I hate it when she struggles."

"You love her because she is who she is," Dwight noted. "That means you have to take the good with the bad."

"There is no bad when it comes to Maddie."

"Oh, you're so far gone I want to put a leash on you so you don't float away on a cloud of love," Dwight teased, smiling for a moment before sobering. "Other than this, other than me pulling you away from your happy existence, are things going well for you?"

"Things are going perfect. We're happy."

"And the proposal? Was it everything you hoped?"

Nick's lips curved. "It was. She was so ... happy. Things got a little tense after because her father showed up back in town, but we've settled in with George and things seem to be going okay on that front, too. He's not nearly the monster we thought he was. He's not perfect, don't get me wrong, but he's not terrible either."

Dwight's eyebrows winged up. "I think that's a story I'm going to want to hear more about."

"As soon as we're out of here, I'll gladly tell you." Nick lifted his chin as Maddie stood. "Did she have anything?"

"I'm not sure," Maddie answered, wrinkling her nose. "Does the name Big Wally mean anything to you, Dwight?"

Dwight didn't bother to hide his surprise. "Is she saying that Big Wally killed all those women?"

"She's saying that Big Wally has been hanging around a lot and he might have some answers."

"Oh, well ... I guess it can't hurt to ask."

"Who is Big Wally?" Nick asked the obvious question.

"This is technically his territory," Dwight explained. "He's known by everyone on these streets."

"He's a gang guy?" Maddie asked.

"Not exactly," Dwight hedged, uncomfortably shifting from one foot to the other. "I think it's better for me to show you than try to explain. He's one of those guys you have to see to believe."

"I don't think I like that sound of that," Nick muttered.

"You haven't seen anything yet," Dwight said. "No matter what you're imagining, it's worse. Trust me. It's so much worse."

6. SIX

"I think you should stay here."

Nick spent the entire drive to Big Wally's home turf trying to think of a way to dissuade Maddie from talking to the man. Dwight didn't say much about Big Wally, but Nick could tell from the taciturn detective's tone that Big Wally wasn't the pleasant sort, as if the moniker and Dwight's original reaction wasn't enough of a tip off. That meant the last thing Nick wanted was for Maddie to come into close proximity with this particular individual.

Maddie kept her face placid as she shifted her eyes to Nick. She sat in the backseat, her eyes trained out the window as they drove, and halfway listened to Nick and Dwight talk in low murmurs. She expected this so she refused to fly off the handle and instead remained calm and collected.

"No."

Nick licked his lips. "Mad, I'm not trying to start a fight but ... um ... I think it's safer if you stay here."

"No." Maddie rubbed her sweaty palms against her knees and shifted her eyes to Dwight. "What can you tell me about this guy?"

Dwight was caught in the middle and he knew it. The looks Nick shot him from the passenger seat were downright evil, but Maddie's expression was so clear, so benevolent, he could never deny her something as simple as answers.

"Big Wally has been around for a good three years or so," Dwight started, ignoring the low growl in the back of Nick's throat. "He started as an enforcer – or that's the rumor, at least – for one of the guys running bets through the casinos. That guy's name was Richard Wood."

"So this Wood guy was a loan shark," Maddie mused, running the new information through her head. "You make it sound as if he's no longer around."

"He's not. Three years ago he was found shot in the back in one of the vacant lots he used to work out of near the casinos," Dwight supplied. "He had a reputation for only allowing those he trusted – and that was a small list, for the record – to get close to him. Rumors abounded that one of his own people killed him."

"What do you believe?" Nick asked.

"Well, I happen to be one of the people who believes Big Wally had a hand in his boss's demise," Dwight replied. "He went from being an enforcer to running book and no one could figure out where he got the money to start his new business."

"You think he stole it from Richard Wood," Nick surmised.

"Pretty much. We can't prove it, though. Absolutely no one will give up information on Wally. On top of that, he's spread his interests to other things – like prostitution and drugs – so he's extended his reach. As of right now, Wally is one of the biggest names on the street."

"I get that and realize I'm out of my element, but why would Wally be hanging out in the lot where a bunch of bodies were dumped if he wasn't involved?" Nick questioned. "That seems like a stupid way to go about running an illegal operation."

"Maybe he was simply conducting business," Maddie suggested, rubbing her forehead as Dwight parked at a well-lit corner. "Maybe he had no idea someone else was dumping bodies in the lot. Maybe our killer picked that lot in the first place because Wally was doing business there."

Intrigued, Dwight put his cruiser in park and shifted so he could face Maddie. "What do you mean?"

Maddie shrugged, taken aback by his serious turn. "It's just ... um ... you said it yourself," she started. "You said that everyone knew Big Wally was running this particular area so they most likely wouldn't mess with him. You've gone out of your way to refrain from talking about his nature, but I can fill in the gaps and I'm pretty sure he's violent and mean because he has to be to keep his soldiers in line.

"He would also have to be that way if he wanted to maintain control," she continued. "He saw what happened when he took out Richard Wood, the gap that created in the power structure, and wants to make sure that doesn't happen to him. That means adopting a brutal persona."

"You're pretty smart sometimes," Dwight noted. "You shouldn't know anything about this world, but you understand it all the same. I'm impressed, Maddie."

"Yes, we're both impressed," Nick drawled. "I still think you should wait in the car, Mad."

"Well, that's not how things are going to work." Maddie's voice was prim, proper, and full of ice. "I need to go with you to get a feeling for the man. Besides, if he is a killer, the likelihood that at least one of his victims might be hanging around is too tempting to ignore."

Nick balked. "You can't start talking to ghosts in front of this guy, Maddie. You'll tip him off that we're up to something and that's the last thing we want."

Maddie rolled her eyes so hard Dwight had to bite the inside of his cheek to keep from laughing.

"Oh, I never would've guessed that, Nicky," Maddie drawled. "I have no intention of talking to ghosts in front of him. I do want to see if any are present, though. I also want to see if I can get a read on him. You seem to forget that I can do more than talk to ghosts. Under the right circumstances, I can also get a few psychic flashes."

"Oh, I remember." Nick was deeply unhappy as he shifted his eyes to look out the windshield. He wasn't used to constant fights with Maddie and found he didn't like her present attitude one bit. Other couples seemed to engage in arguments because it kept the relationship fire burning bright. Nick knew he would never be one of those people and he was downright uncomfortable with the constant arguments. "I've been with you several times when you woke up screaming because of them."

Maddie let loose with a heavy sigh as she reached forward and rested her hand on Nick's shoulder. "I'm sorry. I have to see him to know, though. You'll be with me. I promise it will be okay."

Nick absently ran his fingers over Maddie's but remained silent.

"It will be fine," Dwight agreed, causing Nick to turn in the grave police detective's direction. "I have two patrol cars doing a run right now." He inclined his chin and pointed. "I called before we headed in this direction. You can see them over there."

Nick followed Dwight's gaze. "Doesn't that hurt our position?"

Dwight shrugged. "Not really. Big Wally is used to our presence on his turf. He's turned it into something of a game and gets off from our interactions because he thinks he's getting away with something. He's essentially the most insecure pimp you're ever going to meet. He needs constant validation. For some reason, talking to us makes him think that he's getting validation."

"I don't know what to make of that," Nick said after a beat, giving Maddie's fingers a squeeze before releasing them. "Maddie isn't going to give up on this, though, so we have no choice but to go with her. I'd rather get it done now than wait it out."

"Then let's do it." Dwight mustered a bright smile. "Don't worry about this guy attacking in the middle of the day. He's too smart for that and, like I said, he gets off on the game. He's going to be smug and full of himself, but he won't be aggressive. We've been dealing with this guy for years. I know how he'll react to things. Trust me."

Nick wanted to trust Dwight. He liked the man a great deal. Since Maddie's safety was his primary concern, though, he refused to simply accept easy answers.

"Let's get this over with," Nick said. "The faster we talk to Big Wally, the faster we can put him in our rearview mirror."

Dwight nodded. "Let's get it done."

MADDIE'S ENTIRE KNOWLEDGE of pimps and loan sharks came from movies. She wasn't sure what she expected when she rounded the corner – Nick and Dwight making sure to keep her safely ensconced between them as they entered the lot – but the sight of the absolutely huge man sitting in a recliner in the middle of an overgrown municipal lot was not what she envisioned.

"What the ... ?" Maddie pulled up short as she furrowed her brow. "I don't understand what he's doing."

Dwight followed her gaze, his lips curving. "That's Big Wally."

"I understand that," Maddie said. "It's just he's so ... big."

Big Wally was indeed big. By Nick's estimate, he weighed a good six hundred pounds, wore a sable fedora that was straight out of the Indiana Jones playbook, and rested a pair of lined Crocs on the recliner's footstool as he balanced a tray of what looked to be cookies on his huge gut. His hair was dark, his eyes keen, and even though it wasn't hot there was a thin line of perspiration clinging to his upper lip. He was simply unforgettable. There was no other way to describe him.

Maddie pulled up short in front of the man, her eyes going wide. "Why do you have a recliner in the middle of an empty lot?"

Big Wally focused on the lithe blond rather than her traveling partners. "Every king has a throne. This just happens to be mine."

Dumbfounded, Maddie shifted her eyes around the lot. Big Wally had security in place – at least ten armed men spread themselves around the fence – but none of them moved to converge on their boss. It was clear this wasn't the first time Big Wally had faced off with a police presence and no one looked to be in a mood to panic and cause a scene.

Maddie wasn't particularly worried about Big Wally – his scent was the most offensive thing about him as far as she could tell – so she didn't back down. "Your throne is a recliner?"

Big Wally nodded, his eyes roaming Maddie's body in a manner that made Nick uncomfortable. "Can you think of a better throne?"

Maddie nodded without hesitation. "I'm a big fan of that one on *Game of Thrones*."

"Yes, but I prefer a soft landing," Big Wally noted. "This is a soft landing. If you don't believe me, you can share the chair with me and check it out for yourself."

It took everything Maddie had not to sneer. "I'm good. Thanks."

"Suit yourself." Big Wally's gaze lingered on Maddie's breasts before briefly touching Nick and ultimately landing on Dwight. "Detective Kincaid. It's been a long time."

"Not that long." Dwight kept a polite expression on his face but purposely adopted a relaxed stance. "How are things going, Wally?"

Big Wally shrugged, noncommittal. "You know how it is on the streets. Things are up. Things are down. You have normal swings and abnormal ones. The only thing you can say with any regularity is that tomorrow is another day and things will probably be different."

"I take it to mean that things are down right now," Dwight said.

"Things are ... fine." Big Wally's gaze was back on Maddie. "Who is your friend?"

"She's just a tourist," Dwight replied easily. He had no intention of allowing Big Wally to learn Maddie's identity. While he wasn't as worried about Maddie's safety as Nick – and often thought the younger police officer was something of a whiner when it came to his girlfriend – he was worried enough about Maddie to take proper precautions. "She wanted to meet a big deal operator in the city so I immediately thought of you."

Big Wally preened under the compliment. "I am a big deal. I'm glad to see you acknowledge that."

Maddie wasn't used to watching Dwight appease egos – especially when it came to self-avowed criminals – so she was fascinated by the exchange. That fascination turned into outright horror when she realized Big Wally was digging into a small bag at the side of his chair. When he returned with a needle and what looked to be a bottle of clear liquid, she thought there was a legitimate chance she might lose her footing due to shock.

"What are you doing?" The question was out of Maddie's mouth before she could think better of it. "You're not going to shoot up out here in front of the police, are you?"

Nick licked his lips as he pressed his hand to the small of Maddie's back. "That's insulin, love," he whispered.

"Oh." Realization dawned on Maddie and she felt like an idiot. "I didn't realize ... um ... I'm sorry. I ... well ... I'll just move over here a little bit and let Detective Kincaid ask his questions."

Maddie's cheeks burned as she moved away from the small gathering, forcing her eyes away from an amused Big Wally as Nick ran his thumb over his bottom lip in an attempt to keep from laughing. It was a surreal situation but there was something funny about it and he knew they would be laughing for years to come about Maddie's reaction to Big Wally and his bag of tricks.

"You have questions, Detective Kincaid?" Big Wally turned a thoughtful expression to Dwight. "I guess I should've known this wasn't a social call."

"I do have questions," Dwight confirmed, turning serious. "I'm guessing you heard about the body dump down that way." He gestured vaguely. "It's been brought to our attention that you do a fair bit of a business in that lot."

Instead of reacting with worry or denials, Big Wally snorted. "And you think I'm killing women and dumping them in a place where I do business? That doesn't sound like a smart plan, and we both know I only operate in a smart manner."

"That's exactly what I was thinking," Dwight fired back without hesitation. "In fact, I'm starting to wonder if someone dumped the bodies in the lot simply to frame you."

Nick recognized what Dwight was doing from the start and couldn't help being impressed. The older police officer had managed to stroke Big Wally's ego and make him out to be a victim within the same conversation. It was a smart move.

"I hadn't even considered that." Big Wally shifted on his chair, his countenance serious. "That kind of makes sense in a weird way, doesn't it? I would be the easiest suspect if and when those bodies were found. It gives the real culprit a chance to get away."

"It does," Dwight agreed. "I need to know if your people ever saw anyone odd hanging around there."

"You're going to have to give me more than 'odd.' Everyone who hangs in this area has a few quirks. You know that."

"I do, but we're talking about a serial killer," Dwight pointed out. "He has to be familiar with the area and he's been dumping bodies there for months. Are you sure you didn't see any of the bodies?"

"From what I understand, the bodies were discovered toward the back of the lot," Big Wally noted. "We stayed at the front and didn't explore. We didn't see the need."

"What about the smell, though?" Nick challenged. "You must have picked up on that. There were twenty decomposing bodies practically stacked on top of each other."

"I understand, but it was winter," Big Wally explained. "We didn't spend a lot of time there during the cold months, and down here the cold months are November through March. We're just now starting to spend more time outside. Up until now we've made quick stops but no lingering visits."

"I hadn't considered that." Nick rubbed the back of his neck. "I still don't understand how no one saw those bodies. How were they hidden?"

"The lot was overgrown and there were empty and rotting wooden pallets stacked to the north side," Dwight volunteered. "The bodies were hidden beneath and behind the pallets. No one bothered to check out the area because it was simply assumed there was nothing of worth hidden under a pile of garbage."

"I should point out that I rarely spend time on that lot," Big Wally added. "I do a few stopovers here and there, but it's hardly as if I was hanging out there for more than a minute or two each night. I didn't bother to look around because I had better things to do."

"Would you have called it in if you did know?" Nick asked.

Big Wally shrugged. "It's far more likely I would've had one of my associates make an anonymous call. Believe me, no one wants a serial killer working his way through women on our turf. It creates issues and we're not the sort of men who want issues."

Nick could believe that. "So you're claiming you didn't see or know anything about this?"

"I don't traffic in killing," Big Wally replied. "I traffic in other vices, don't get me wrong, but there's no profit in killing."

"So where does that leave us?" Nick asked, sliding his eyes to Dwight.

Dwight shrugged. "Exactly where we were. In fact ... ." He didn't get a chance to finish because Big Wally took everyone by surprise when he jumped to his feet – a movement that was much quicker than his size should've allowed – and extended a hand in Maddie's direction.

"Hey, girl! Where do you think you're going?"

Nick snapped his head toward Maddie and widened his eyes when he realized she was walking toward a large semi-trailer parked on the one-way street at the back of the lot. "Maddie?"

Maddie didn't answer, instead shuffling toward the trailer and resting her hand on the cool metal.

"Get her away from there, Kincaid!" Big Wally howled, his face flushed with color. "I didn't invite her to touch my things."

Dwight was instantly alert. "And what are you worried about her finding?"

"Nothing." Big Wally tugged on his shirt but it was too small to cover his large gut. "I just don't want her touching my things."

Dwight didn't believe that for a second. He lifted a warning finger in Big Wally's direction before taking a step toward the intent blond. "What do you have, Maddie?"

Maddie's expression was grave. "There are people inside that truck ... and they're crying."

Dwight licked his lips as Big Wally shifted from one foot to the other.

"She's lying," Big Wally offered lamely.

"Yeah, well, we're going to need you to open that truck all the same," Dwight said. "You'd better hope she's mistaken because otherwise, well, you're going to be in a whole heap of trouble."

Big Wally's face twisted. "I want my lawyer."

"That can be arranged."

7. SEVEN

Nick hurried to Maddie's side, keeping a wary eye on Big Wally's men as he closed the distance. They looked confused, their eyes wide as they waited for guidance. Big Wally was clearly upset, but his soldiers had been with him long enough to know that he would frown upon attacking cops. Ultimately the decision was taken out of their hands, though, because the backup Dwight called for before entering the lot swooped in with guns drawn the second he alerted them to a forthcoming issue.

The police officers yelled warnings and orders, and when Nick was certain they had Big Wally's men under control – Dwight was grappling with the man in charge in the center of things – Nick turned his full attention to Maddie.

"What are you doing?" Nick hissed, keeping his voice low.

"There are people inside of this truck." Maddie ran her hands over the cool metal, her face twisting. "We have to get it open."

"Okay, Mad, we'll get it open." Nick was befuddled. "How do you know there are people inside?"

"Because a young girl told me."

Nick glanced around, his confusion deepening. "What girl?"

"She died inside the truck."

The weight of Maddie's words slammed into Nick's stomach like a fist. "Oh. Crap. I ... just crap. Hold on."

Even though he didn't want to leave her, Nick swiveled and searched the sea of faces converging on the lot. Dwight called for significantly more backup than Nick initially realized because cops appeared to be flooding the square expanse, making for a lot more uniformed officers than could fit into two patrol cars. Nick ignored them as he tried to get Dwight's attention.

After a few more seconds of arguing with Big Wally, Dwight ordered one of the uniformed officers to cuff him and then strode toward Nick with a worried look etched on his face.

"What is going on?" Dwight asked, keeping his voice low. "This is about to blow up into a really big mess and I need to know what's happening."

"The truck." Nick gestured helplessly. "Maddie says there are people locked in the truck."

"How does she know that? I didn't hear anything."

"She says at least one of the people in the truck is dead and that girl's ghost told her."

"Oh, well, great." Dwight made a face that would've been humorous under different circumstances. "I can't wait to say that a ghost is giving us information."

"Just say that Maddie heard something." Nick was grim. "We have to get that truck open because if we don't, Maddie is going to do it herself and ... yup, there she goes." Nick slapped his hand to his forehead when Maddie moved to the back of the trailer and began fumbling with the latch.

"Oh, geez." Dwight broke into a run so he could get to Maddie before she lifted the lever. "Let me do it, Maddie."

"I've got it." Maddie made grunting noises as she struggled to lift the heavy door.

"No." Dwight slapped Maddie's hands away, causing her to widen her eyes. "I need to do it, Maddie." Dwight opted to be pragmatic. "If you do it, we might run into problems with evidence chains down the line. Trust me. I'll do it."

"Oh, well, okay." Maddie took a step back but none of the tension vacated her shoulders.

"Hold on." Dwight exchanged a weighted look with Nick and then gripped the handle on the door. "Here we go."

In the back of his head, Dwight couldn't help but wonder if Maddie was exaggerating ... or even somehow mistaken. He'd seen her in action and she was phenomenal. She'd turned him from a man who didn't believe in the paranormal to a diehard believer. What he found inside the trailer, though, was enough to shake him to his very core.

The truck was full of young women and girls. They all looked to be under the age of twenty-five, their faces streaked with tears and dirt. Most of them scrambled away from the influx of light and Dwight knew he would never forget the pathetic whimpering sound the women made as they huddled together as a form of protection.

"Oh, my ... ." Words escaped him.

"Son of a ... ." Nick took a step away from Maddie and peered into the trailer. "What is going on here?"

"Nothing good," Dwight replied, his stomach threatening to revolt at the stench inside the truck. He held up his hands in what he hoped was an innocent and nonthreatening manner. "Ladies, my name is Dwight Kincaid. I'm a detective with the Detroit Police Department. You're safe. I want you to know that. I ... ." He had no idea how to continue.

Nick was out of his element and all he could do was watch the determined police detective struggle to find the correct words to help the situation. To his utter surprise, Maddie pushed past him and placed herself at the end of the of the trailer.

"You don't have to be afraid." Maddie's voice was strong and clear. "We're going to help you. You're not going to be trapped here any longer. We need you to come out, though."

A murmur went through the women. Nick counted in his head. There had to be at least twenty of them, and that didn't include the two prone bodies at the back of the trailer. They were covered with tarps and didn't appear to be moving. He considered hopping into the trailer to see if they were alive, but he knew that would traumatize the women even further.

Maddie was decisive when she turned to Dwight. "We need more women here. They're afraid. They've obviously been mistreated."

"I can place a call." Dwight forced himself to remain calm as he dug into his pocket for his phone.

"Call for medical personnel, too," Maddie instructed. "The more women the better. We need water and food. These women are clearly dehydrated and emaciated." She turned her head to the side for a moment, staring at something only she could see. Nick was convinced it was the ghost who led her to the trailer even though he couldn't see the girl. "We also need the medical examiner," Maddie said after a beat. "There are two bodies in the back."

Dwight rested his hand on Maddie's shoulder. "I'm on it right now. See if you can talk to them. We need to get them out of that trailer and it would be better if we didn't have to forcibly remove them. That's only going to traumatize them further."

Maddie nodded. "Okay. I ... ." She didn't get a chance to finish her thought because that was the moment Big Wally decided to start bellowing.

"I want my lawyer right now!" he shrieked. "I'm going to own all of your badges before this is said and done."

The look Maddie shot him as she turned, hands on hips, was straight out of a horror movie. "This isn't about you."

Big Wally snagged her gaze, an evil ripple passing through him as he glared. "Oh, this is about me. This is my turf. Everything that happens here is about me."

"Including human trafficking?" Nick asked angrily.

"Human trafficking?" Big Wally sputtered. "I think you're confused. That trailer is merely a place for my girls to take a rest between shifts."

"So you're owning up to prostitution but not to illegally holding these women?" Maddie challenged.

Big Wally shrugged, unbothered. "I'm very clearly not a prostitute. You can't pin that on me."

"No, you're right," Maddie said dryly. "You would have to pay someone double – actually probably triple – to sleep with you so no one would ever mistake you for a prostitute."

Big Wally's eyes narrowed until they were nothing more than glittery slits. "You're going to want to tread carefully, girlie. I don't know who you are, but I realize this is all your fault. You're not going to like what happens once my lawyer gets here."

"Don't you even think about threatening her," Nick warned.

Big Wally ignored him and remained focused on Maddie. "You've fouled things up and I won't forget it."

"Oh, please," Maddie scoffed, rolling her eyes. "The only foul thing here is you. You get your power by hurting others. I'm not afraid of you. I'm never going to be afraid of you. So shut your mouth, swallow that hot air you like to expel because you think you're a big deal, and worry about your own future. You're not a part of what's going to happen to these women."

"Those women are my property."

Maddie let loose with a derisive snort. "I can't help but wonder whose property you're going to be when you're locked up in prison for the rest of your life. I wonder how aggressive your cellmate will be."

"You have no idea who you're dealing with," Big Wally seethed.

"No, you have no idea who you're dealing with," Maddie shot back. "Now ... go away. I'm done talking to you." She turned her back on Big Wally and focused on the nearest girl. She looked to be young, not even eighteen yet, and Maddie offered up a kind smile as she extended her hand. "I know it's hard, but I need you to trust me. We're going to help you. Have faith. The good guys are here and they're going to make things better."

The girl eyed Maddie for what felt like forever and Nick held his breath waiting for a response. Finally, the girl held out a tentative hand and didn't so much as flinch when her fingers touched Maddie's welcoming grip.

"Good." Maddie beamed. "Everything is going to be okay. I promise we'll help you get through this."

. . .

"I CAN'T BELIEVE HER."

Nick stood next to Dwight two hours later, weariness emanating from his very bones as he watched Maddie with the women. It took almost a full hour to get everybody out of the truck, but Maddie refused to leave the front of the vehicle until every girl was freed.

That's when the paramedics and mental health professionals took over. Even then, though, Maddie refused to walk away. Instead she sat with the women, offered support and as many answers as she could supply, and steadily worked her way through the crowd.

"I can't believe her either," Dwight admitted, admiration practically rolling off him. "I always knew she was special but ... she's grown to be a remarkable woman."

"If another man said that to me, I would consider punching him," Nick admitted. "Since you love her like a daughter, though, I'm going to let it slide."

Dwight snorted. "She's stronger than she was. I used to worry about her like you wouldn't believe. I thought there was a very real chance the world would swallow her whole at some point and there would be nothing I could do about it.

"When she first returned to Blackstone Bay, I honestly thought that was what would happen," he continued. "Instead she found her way back to you and she's stronger than she's ever been. You did that for her."

"No." Nick immediately started shaking his head. "She's always been strong. She just never realized it. She was afraid to admit who she was and that made her appear weak simply because she didn't want to rock the boat. She's not frightened to be who she is any longer and that allows her to be who she was always meant to be."

"She's not frightened because of you. You accepted her secret and loved her despite it. You played your part in this."

"I've loved her from the moment I saw her. Sure, it was in kindergarten and I was convinced she was some sort of angel, but I've always loved her. I don't feel the way I do despite what she is. I love her because of who she is. It's always been there."

Dwight cocked his head. "Aw. You're kind of a schmaltzy romantic. You know that, right?"

Nick shrugged. "What can I say? She brings it out in me."

"She brings out the best in everyone," Dwight agreed, shifting his eyes to the patrol car where Big Wally stood, his hands cuffed behind his back, and talked to his lawyer in a low voice. The arresting police officers refused to let him wander around, but they moved far enough away that Big Wally could have some privacy. "He's clearly not happy with what the lawyer is telling him."

Nick followed Dwight's gaze. "Definitely not," he agreed. "What's going on there?"

"Wally wants to avoid being transported to lockup, but we've made it clear that's not going to happen," Dwight replied. "He claims that the women weren't being held captive and they wanted to be in the trailer."

"I have trouble believing that." Nick's anger was palpable. "Two of them were dead."

"Yes, we pointed that out."

"And?"

"And nothing." Dwight scratched at the side of his nose, weariness threatening to catch up with him. "He's not going to get away with it even though he has a high-priced suit for an attorney. I'm not worried about the charges sticking, although I'm going to need to take Maddie's statement."

Nick recognized the uncomfortable look on Dwight's face. "I'll talk to her. In fact, I'll get her now and have a discussion before we sit down with you."

If anything, Dwight's discomfort only grew. "I can't take her statement because of our relationship. People understand that I'm close to her. That means someone else is going to have to take her statement."

"Oh." Realization dawned on Nick. "I'll take care of it. I'll make sure she knows exactly what to say."

"Good. While you're gathering her, I'll grab Annette Winston.

She's a good detective and she won't go out of her way to make Maddie uncomfortable. Hopefully this won't be too painful."

Nick understood exactly what Dwight was worried about. "I'm sure it will be fine. Maddie will understand."

"I hope so."

Nick bobbed his head before sliding around a group of medical personnel. They were calm and matter-of-fact when working with the women. It would be a long night for everyone concerned, though. Nick had no doubt about that.

He waited at the edge of the action until he caught Maddie's eye and then inclined his chin to get her to come to him. She furrowed her brow before whispering something to the girl in front of her. Then she politely distanced herself from the group and joined Nick.

"I wanted to check on you." Nick linked his fingers with Maddie's and dragged her to a spot away from everyone else. He wanted to make sure they were out of earshot. "How are you feeling?"

Maddie shrugged, noncommittal. "I'm not sure how to feel," Maddie admitted. "I'm glad we found them, don't get me wrong, but I wanted to believe ugliness like this didn't exist. When I lived down here, it was hard to ignore the terrible things I saw. When I moved back to Blackstone Bay, though, it was easier to put the hateful nature of evildoers behind me because they were rarer up there thanks to the smaller population base."

Nick couldn't hold back a wry grin. "You've almost died several times since returning to Blackstone Bay. Ugly things happen there, too."

"I know, but you're in Blackstone Bay and you make the world a prettier place."

"Oh, so cute." Nick poked Maddie's side before pulling her in for a hug. "I'm sorry you had to see this, love, but I'm awfully glad you were here. You were the only one who could get through to those women and give them a glimmer of hope. They trusted you right from the start."

"I'm not sure about that."

"I am. You saved them, Maddie." Nick pulled back to search her face. "You were a hero today."

"I don't feel like much of a hero. Two of those girls are dead. I didn't save them."

"I heard the medical examiner talking," Nick argued. "They've been dead for at least twenty-four hours. They were dead before we hit town. There was absolutely nothing you could do to save them."

"I know that in my head. My heart, though, my heart keeps putting up a fight."

"Well, you can't do the impossible, Mad. Even you aren't capable of that." Nick pressed a kiss to her forehead as he swayed back and forth. "You have to answer some questions from the police. You know that, right?"

Maddie didn't stiffen or pull away. "I'm well aware."

"Dwight can't be the one to question you. It won't look right."

"I know that, too."

"I ... ." Nick broke off and licked his lips.

"I know what you're worried about, Nicky." Maddie's tone was even. "I'm going to say I heard something in the truck and that's what drew me to it, a whimper through the walls so to speak. I understand I can't mention ghosts or psychic visions. It's going to be okay."

Nick pursed his lips as he glanced down at her beautiful face. "You always manage to take me by surprise. Here I was worried that you might melt down or not understand and you're already two steps ahead of me."

"Believe it or not, I've had to do this sort of thing before." Maddie turned grim. "At least this time we had a mostly happy ending."

"We did indeed." Nick smoothed her hair. "Let's get this over with. After that, I'll take you to dinner."

"That sounds like a plan. I'm ready."

Nick had no doubt that she was. Dwight was right, he realized. Maddie was stronger than she had any right being. He couldn't help being unbelievably proud. She'd grown into a fantastic woman and she belonged to him.

What more could he possibly want?

8. EIGHT

Maddie and Nick went back to Mexicantown for dinner. It was close and neither of them wanted to wander too far out of their comfort zone. Dwight was hungry and exhausted, but he was forced to remain on scene. With little else to do, Maddie suggested picking up ice cream for the women she knew were to be transported to the hospital where she used to work and serving as something of a personal delivery service.

Because he was curious about the life Maddie led while away from him, Nick readily agreed.

They delivered ice cream to a few familiar faces – all of which seemed surprised and delighted to see Maddie again – and once she hit the ward and made her presence known, several of Maddie's former co-workers – she worked as a nurse in the same hospital for years – hurried to the fifth floor to greet her.

"I can't believe you're back," Iris Banfield gushed, throwing her arms around Maddie and offering up an effusive hug. "We've missed you so much."

"We have," Sandy Littleton agreed, nodding sagely. "It's hell getting people who actually want to work in this place. They all seem to go to other hospitals."

"Oh, well, that's nice of you to say," Maddie hedged, her cheeks flushing with a mixture of pleasure and embarrassment. "I've missed you guys, too."

"When is your first shift?" Iris asked.

Maddie balked. "I'm not back to work," she replied hurriedly. "I'm just back for a visit. I happened to be downtown when the women were found in the back of that truck and since I saw and talked to a few of them, I wanted to drop off a treat."

"Oh, you were the one who made an ice cream run." Sandy furrowed her brow. "I heard whispers about that, too. That was nice of you."

"I'm still disappointed you're not coming back," Iris said. Maddie remembered the woman as a hard worker and blunt talker and she was one of the few people Maddie legitimately missed once she returned to Blackstone Bay. "I was excited when I heard you were here."

"Oh, well ... I hate to disappoint you, but I'm not coming back." Maddie was sheepish as Nick slipped an arm around her shoulders.

"I guess we know why you're not coming back." Sandy gave Nick a lingering look. "And who are you?"

"Oh, I'm sorry, I've forgotten my manners." Maddie stirred. "This is Nick Winters. He's my ... fiancé." The word felt weird slipping off Maddie's tongue but it also felt right. "We're getting married."

"That's generally what *fiancé* means," Iris drawled, making a clucking sound with her tongue. "Good grief. He's a tall drink of water, isn't he?"

Maddie had never understood that expression, but she nodded all the same. "He's all that and a bag of chips."

Nick made an odd face, but Iris and Sandy burst into hysterical gales of laughter.

"Oh, I forgot that joke," Iris said, her cheeks burning with happiness as she bent over at the waist and fought to contain her mirth. "We beat that joke for months."

"What joke?" Nick asked, genuinely curious. He enjoyed meeting Maddie's former co-workers because it gave him hope. All the stories she told about her time away indicated a lonely existence. Iris and

Sandy's boisterous attitudes seemed to indicate that Maddie had at least two people to talk to. That made him feel much better.

"It was a thing," Maddie said. "There was a doctor here who thought he was God's gift to women and he once mentioned to a new nurse that he was all that and a bag of chips and we couldn't stop laughing about it."

"It's an in-joke," Sandy added. "Sorry. I didn't remember it until Maddie mentioned it."

"I honestly forgot it until it was already on the tip of my tongue," Maddie said. "Please tell me he's gone."

Iris shook her head, turning solemn. "No, and he's even more full of himself since you left. I don't think he got over the fact that you wouldn't stay even though he practically begged you to do it."

Maddie inadvertently stiffened when she felt Nick shift next to her. "Oh, well ... ."

"He asked you to stay?" Nick cocked an eyebrow. "It seems I'm missing more to the story than I thought."

"It's nothing," Maddie said hurriedly. "I swear it's not. It's just ... he tried to get everyone on the nursing staff to date him. He seemed to think it was a game of sorts. That's the only reason he wanted me to stay."

"That's not the only reason," Sandy countered, clearly missing the look of distress on Maddie's face. "He was always panting after you because ... well, you're you ... and he thought he would have time to wear down your defenses. That never happened and he really pulled out the stops when he realized you were leaving. It was almost comical the way he followed you around."

"I found it funny," Iris agreed. "He was a bitter man for the first two weeks after you left. He kept asking if we'd heard from you and didn't believe us when we said we hadn't."

"I'm sorry about that." Maddie meant it. "Once I got home, though, there was a lot going on."

Iris slid a sidelong look to Nick. "I can see that. In fact, I'm pretty sure I remember this guy from that framed photograph you had in your apartment. You only had like three decorations, and that photograph was one of them. He looked a lot younger in the picture but ... this is him, isn't it?"

Maddie nodded. "This is my Nicky."

"Well, Nicky, I see why she decided to go home," Iris purred with flirtatious delight. "We thought it was a mistake when she announced it, but her mind was made up. She said her granny needed her. I'm starting to think that was only half the story, though. You're clearly the other half."

"And I definitely needed her," Nick agreed, keeping his hand on Maddie's back as he rolled the new information through his head. He wanted answers but he knew better than questioning Maddie in front of her former co-workers. "While I'm sure it's not a popular opinion here, I'm glad she's home."

"Honey, if I had you waiting for me I'd move to the middle of nowhere, too," Iris drawled, causing Nick to let loose with a sly grin. "Screw work. I would just sit around and watch you flex for hours upon hours."

Maddie pressed her lips together to keep from laughing, but Nick belted out a loud chuckle.

"That's what Maddie does when we're home. She stares at me and drools."

"I do not!" Maddie playfully slapped Nick's arms. "You'll give them the wrong idea if you say things like that."

"I don't think anyone can get the wrong idea when seeing you two together," Sandy said. "I mean ... you make small town living look so very good."

"We hope so." Nick ran his knuckles up and down Maddie's back, relaxing into the conversation as Maddie, Iris, and Sandy talked about changes to the hospital. After a few moments, he let his attention drift and his gaze landed on a sour looking man standing next to the elevator. He wore a physician's coat and a stethoscope around his neck, but the look on his face was cold and aloof. At first Nick thought he was agitated by the noise and hoopla surrounding Maddie. After a few minutes, though, Nick realized the man was staring at Maddie with such intensity that it bordered on antagonistic.

"Who is that, love?" Nick asked, inclining his chin in the man's direction.

Maddie kept her hand up so Iris and Sandy could "ooh" and "aah" over her engagement ring and looked in the direction he indicated. The smile she'd been boasting instantly fled. "That's Dr. Milton Tipton." Maddie's lips curled into a sneer. "He's got a few ... issues."

"He's the doctor we were talking about," Iris supplied. "He's the one who kept asking Maddie out when he found out she was leaving."

"He must've heard you were down here," Sandy noted. "He probably wanted to see you and took a step back when he realized you weren't alone."

Instinctively, Nick tightened his grip on Maddie. "That's him, huh?"

Tipton looked to be in his late forties, perhaps early fifties, and his gaze was so intent Nick couldn't help but wonder if he was trying to telepathically connect with Maddie from across the room.

"I don't like him," Nick announced, causing Maddie to purse her lips and Sandy and Iris to giggle uncontrollably. "He's staring at you and it makes me uncomfortable."

"Don't make a thing about it," Maddie warned, keeping her voice low. "This is a hospital and we might need to come back and talk to those women at some point. He could make it difficult for us."

Nick wasn't sure he cared about that, but he knew Maddie did so he reined in his temper. "Fine. I won't say anything. We should probably get out of here, though."

Maddie shared the sentiment. "Yeah. I want to run by the building where my old apartment was just for nostalgia's sake and then I thought we could head back to the hotel. There's nothing more we can do tonight."

"That sounds like a plan to me." Nick kept his left hand on Maddie's waist and forced a charming smile for Iris and Sandy. "It was a great pleasure to meet both of you."

"Oh, the pleasure was all ours," Iris deadpanned, snickering.

"Maybe we can figure out a time to have lunch while I'm here," Maddie suggested. "I'll text you tomorrow when I know more."

Sandy brightened. "That sounds like a plan."

Maddie was distinctly uncomfortable as she and Nick moved toward the elevator. She could feel Tipton's eyes on her and she didn't like the way her skin crawled thanks to his unwanted attention.

"I'll probably sleep ten hours tonight," Maddie offered, letting loose with a smile that looked more like a grimace than anything else when Tipton caught her gaze. "Hello, Dr. Tipton."

"Miss Graves." Tipton's voice was gravelly. "I didn't realize you were back working here."

"I just stopped in for a visit." Maddie shifted closer to Nick. "We're leaving, though."

"I can see that."

"I'm Nick Winters." Nick extended his hand, but Tipton ignored it.

"Well, it was nice that you stopped in for a visit, Ms. Graves." Tipton pushed himself away from the wall. "I hope you have a pleasant visit."

Nick and Maddie watched him go in silence, waiting until they were safely on the elevator to speak.

"He seems nice," Nick offered. "He should be one of the commentators on *The View* or something."

Maddie broke into hysterical giggles. "He's always been that way. It's like hanging out with the crypt keeper."

"Well, I can't wait to hear about him hitting on you during our trip to your old apartment," Nick said, causing Maddie's smile to slip. "I think you might've left a few things out when you told me about your time down here."

"It was nothing, Nicky. It wasn't a big deal."

"I'll be the judge of that."

IT REALLY WASN'T a big deal. It seemed Dr. Tipton asked Maddie out five times, but she never said yes and did her best to let him down easy so as not to negatively affect their working relationship. Nick wasn't happy to think about the unfriendly man drooling over his fiancée, but ultimately it was hardly something to concern himself with. Still, that didn't mean he didn't enjoy teasing Maddie over the entire kerfuffle.

"So you like me better, right?" Nick queried as he followed Maddie into a quiet apartment building located two blocks down the road from the hospital. "You're not regretting your choice, are you?"

"Ha, ha." Maddie rolled her eyes. "That's not even remotely funny."

"I wasn't trying to be funny. It was an honest question." Nick shifted his eyes to the front door of the apartment complex – it was one of those old Detroit hotels they'd converted into communal living quarters – and frowned when he saw the weak lock. "Please tell me this was better when you lived here."

Maddie glanced at the lock. "I'm pretty sure it's exactly the same."

"Ugh. It's so good that I didn't know what kind of place you were living in," Nick groused. "If Olivia had shown me photos of this place – or even mentioned how bad it was – I don't care how angry I was at you, I would've been down here in a shot to steal you away."

Maddie chuckled as she climbed the steps that led to the second floor. "I wonder how that would've changed things if you did that."

"Oh, we both know I would've started yelling and then I would've crumbled in five seconds flat and we would've been all over each other inside thirty minutes."

"Hmm. That sounds rather intriguing."

"It does," Nick agreed. "I promise to be all over you as soon as we get back to the hotel room to make up for not coming after you sooner. How does that sound?"

"Like a good way to put this day behind us." Maddie was sincere as she slipped her hand in his. "I'm afraid I'm going to have nightmares tonight. I accidentally brushed up against a few minds when I was helping those girls and ... well ... it wasn't pretty."

"I'll be with you," Nick promised. "In fact, I bought some melatonin because I anticipated you might have trouble sleeping. Since you won't take anything heavier than cold medicine, I thought that was the way to go."

"You are a genius." Maddie beamed as she hit the top of the stairs, her lips curving down at the sight of the dingy hallway. "Here it is."

Nick's stomach twisted as he glanced around. "Where?"

"Right there. The second apartment on the left."

Nick looked at the apartment she pointed toward. The hallway was dark, boasted a dank quality, and it didn't feel safe. He hated it on sight. "I can't believe you lived here."

"The apartment wasn't so bad," Maddie argued. "It wasn't great, but it wasn't terrible."

"I still don't like it." He wrapped his arms around her waist from behind. "You belong with me."

"I think we both agree with that."

Nick pressed a soft kiss to Maddie's tender neck. "I love you so much, Mad. I don't like to think of you being here without me."

"I don't really think about it much," Maddie admitted. "I just wanted to see it so I could remind myself how much happier I am now. I don't miss this place. You don't have to worry about that."

"Good." Nick gave Maddie a long squeeze before pointing her toward the stairs. "Let's head back to the hotel. I'm ready to put this day behind us."

"You and me both." Maddie's smile was back in place when they hit the main floor, but she pulled up short when she saw an older woman collecting her mail in the small alcove off the front door. "Mrs. Peterson?"

The woman snapped her head in Maddie's direction, furrowing her brow for a long beat before she visibly relaxed. "You're the girl who used to live here, right? The nurse."

Maddie bobbed her head. "That's me. I was just showing my friend the old apartment when I saw you. How are you?"

The woman shrugged. "I'm still alive. I guess that's as good as it gets at my age."

Nick had to press his lips together to keep from laughing at the woman's matter-of-fact attitude.

When Mrs. Peterson shuffled closer, her eyes expressed confusion as she searched Nick's face. "Who are you?"

"This is my fiancé," Maddie answered automatically. "This is Nick."

"You're not the guy who came by right after Maddie left," the woman noted. "You're definitely not that guy."

Maddie had trouble following the conversation. "What guy? Are you saying a guy came by?"

"He was looking for you," Mrs. Peterson volunteered. "It was the day after you left. I don't think he was expecting you to move as fast as you did. He said your last shift at the hospital was the previous day and he wanted to catch you before you left town.

"I told him you left five minutes after your last shift and never looked back," she continued. "That seemed to make him angry and he called me a liar. I don't put up with people being rude – you know that – so I had to call security to kick him out.

"Now, granted, Mike isn't much of a security guard because he spends all his time playing video games in the back office, but he showed up right away and then the guy left," she said. "I thought for sure he was with you, but this guy is not the guy who stopped by so I guess I was wrong on that."

"What did he look like?" Nick asked, suspicious.

"All I know is that he's not you," Mrs. Peterson replied. "I didn't do a sketch of him or anything. Besides, that was a year ago. It was clearly some sort of mistake. You don't have to worry about it or get your girdle in a bunch or anything."

In his head, the words made sense. Still, Nick couldn't shake his sense of dread. "Okay, well, it was nice to meet you. We have to get going."

"Make sure you lock the door on your way out," Mrs. Peterson ordered. "I don't want more riffraff in the building. Are we clear?"

Nick mock saluted. "Crystal."

"I bet you think you're cute," Mrs. Peterson muttered. "You're not, though."

Maddie smiled as she watched the woman ascend the steps. "I think you're cute, Nicky. I've always thought it."

"Good." Nick pushed the worry out of his head. "Let's go to the hotel and be cute together."

"Finally something I want to do."

9. NINE

Maddie dreamed poorly, but Nick was there the entire night to beat back the nightmares. In the end, she got a solid six hours of sleep and didn't feel half bad when they met Dwight for breakfast in the hotel restaurant the next morning.

"You look tired," Maddie announced, concern overwhelming her as she took the seat next to Dwight and rested the back of her hand on his cheek. "Are you okay?"

"You sound like my wife," Dwight complained, shaking his head. "I'm perfectly fine. Lack of sleep never did anyone in so there's no need to fret."

"Didn't the kids in *A Nightmare on Elm Street* go crazy after lack of sleep?" Nick asked.

Dwight scowled. "Oh, you're so funny. You with your full night's sleep and dreamy eyes."

Nick made a face. "Have you been thinking about my dreamy eyes and not telling me?"

"No, but I happened to run into Sage this morning as she was heading toward the shower and I told her you guys were in town and she insisted that she see you before she heads back to school at the end of the weekend," Dwight replied. "Then there was some talk of dreamy eyes and how you're built like a movie star."

Maddie barely swallowed her giggle. "Oh, well, Sage is young. It's perfectly normal for a girl her age to develop a crush on an older man."

"I'm not even nine years older than her," Nick groused. "I'm hardly an older man. I'm nothing like that douche doctor who tried to pick you up." Nick wasn't one for saying rude things in public, but he didn't feel bad about dropping the D-word and he ignored the look on the approaching waitress's face as he ordered coffee. "Mad, what do you want to drink?"

"Coffee, a glass of water, and tomato juice," Maddie replied, offering up a sweet smile for the waitress. The woman didn't look any happier with Maddie's response so Maddie quickly turned serious. "Thank you." She waited until the waitress disappeared to retrieve their drinks and focused on Dwight. "Of course we want to see Sage. I'm worried about you, though. How late were you out?"

"It wasn't that I was out all that late," Dwight replied, rubbing the tender spot between his eyebrows. "It's simply that I was up early because apparently Big Wally decided to cut a deal when he realized he wouldn't be walking free and clear."

Nick straightened. "Really? That's good news. Why didn't you call us?"

"Because it happened before six and I didn't want to wake you. Not everyone needs to go without sleep. Although ... you guys look like you had a good enough night. I'm glad to see that. I was a little worried."

"We're absolutely fine," Maddie said.

Dwight didn't look convinced and turned to Nick. "Really?"

"She had a few bad dreams but nothing compared to what I thought she would have," Nick answered. "Honestly, it wasn't nearly as bad as it could've been. After we left you, though, we took a trip to the hospital so she could drop off ice cream to the girls there and then we ran into a few of her old co-workers."

"Let me guess, Iris and Sandy?"

Nick nodded. "They seemed nice enough. In fact, I was kind of glad to meet them because I always pictured Maddie having no one to talk to while she was down here and it made me sad. She clearly had those two women. They kind of remind me of Christy in a weird way."

"Huh." Maddie tilted her head to the side. "I never really thought about that, but you're right. They are like Christy. Maybe I have a type when it comes to friends."

Nick chuckled. "Since we were friends before we got together, that makes me feel a bit uncomfortable."

"You're different. You're in a classification all your own."

"That's what all the women say," Nick teased, squeezing her hand. "I'm a god amongst men."

The waitress picked that moment to return with their beverages, cocking an eyebrow at Nick's statement before taking their breakfast orders and hurrying away. Nick watched her go, chagrined.

"I'm not on top of my game today," he said after a beat. "That woman is probably licking my toast."

"Probably," Dwight agreed. "Tell me about your visit to the hospital. How were the girls?"

"Quiet and overwhelmed," Maddie replied. "The hospital staff was gentle and tried to put them at ease, but I can tell a lot of them are terrified. They didn't utter a single word."

"Yeah, well, I know why that is." Dwight shifted on his chair. "Some of them are here illegally. In fact, almost all of them are illegals."

"As in illegal aliens?" Maddie knit her eyebrows. "I don't understand why that's important."

"They don't want to talk because they'll be deported," Nick explained. "Most of them took a chance on a better life only to be saddled with debts they'll never be able to pay off by predatory forces. Then they were sold to a slug like Wally and forced into prostitution, probably being told the only way to settle their debts was by selling themselves."

Maddie felt sick to her stomach. "Then what?"

"Then nothing," Dwight answered. "They work until they can't work any longer or they age out to a point where none of the clients want them and then they're either cut loose – which is like a death sentence – or killed to cover up the operation."

All the color drained from Maddie's face. "I don't understand, though. That's the sort of thing we hear about happening in other countries. How could that be happening here without anyone knowing?"

"You would be surprised at the number of things happening here that are downright despicable," Dwight replied. "Remember when I mentioned the proximity to the bridge and human trafficking yesterday?"

"Vaguely. I wasn't paying that much attention because it made me sad."

"Well, that's exactly what we're dealing with here," Dwight said. "Big Wally wasn't talkative at first, but once his attorney realized there was no getting out of this situation, he basically ordered Wally to make a deal."

"What kind of deal?" Nick asked. "What did you give him?"

"More than I would have liked but less than he wanted," Dwight answered. "He wanted to walk away free and clear. As it is, the prosecutor is going to recommend five years."

"Five years!" Maddie almost blew her stack and her voice was shrill enough to draw attention from several nearby tables. "You can't be serious. Two of those girls in the trailer were dead."

"I know." Dwight awkwardly patted her hand in an attempt to calm her. "Don't get all worked up here, Maddie. I have no control over the prosecutor's office."

"But it's not fair," Maddie persisted. "Those girls are dead."

"They are." Dwight looked pained. "They're also Hispanic and not from this country. The prosecutor wasn't moved by their plight because they were here illegally."

"Oh, well, that is ... ." Maddie had no words to express her fury.

"Love, we can't force the prosecutor to do what we want," Nick said quietly. "Even in Blackstone Bay the prosecutor basically does what he wants without any oversight. We've been lucky because he wants to appear tough on crime, but Dwight is in a different position here and he's doing the best he can."

"I'm not blaming Dwight."

"It kind of seems that you are."

"Oh, well, that's not what I meant." Maddie forced herself to relax, although only marginally. "I just don't understand how you can let that animal walk free after only five years. He's ruined lives, and that's only the girls we know about. Do you really think he doesn't have girls stashed elsewhere?"

"I understand your concern, Maddie, but we can only do what we can do and Wally has information on people who are worse than him," Dwight said. "We had to weigh the worth of Wally's information against his punishment. If we can save other girls, then that's what we're going to do."

Mollified, Maddie rubbed her cheek. "Okay. I guess that makes sense. What did he tell you?"

"Well, it was like pulling teeth," Dwight said, leaning back in his chair and extending his long legs as he sipped his coffee. "At first he denied knowledge of the girls being in the truck and tried to blame it on the people who work for him.

"I explained that wasn't going to work because he always boasted how he oversaw everything and that meant he was really lying and in charge of nothing if we were to believe his new story," he continued. "I told him that information would probably be welcomed by the men he'd be serving time with and he changed his tune rather quickly."

"Yeah, I can see that," Nick said. "He needs to be a big man to survive prison, but he can't play the victim game with you if he starts boasting now. He's in a tough spot."

"I hope someone whacks him over the head with his stupid Crocs while he's in prison," Maddie muttered, annoyed.

Nick cracked a smile. "You really need to form an opinion, love. This waffling thing you're doing is ridiculous."

Maddie ignored the jab. "So what did he give you?"

"Well, he gave us a rundown of the operation," Dwight replied. "It's big. It's real big, in fact. It runs between New York to Detroit to Chicago. It's an entire train of human trafficking."

"And it's all for sex?" Maddie asked.

"Not exactly." Dwight dragged a restless hand through his hair. "So, basically what happens is that runners pick up women from the streets. We're talking recent border crossers – which almost always happens in the south because no one from the north wants to bother – and at-risk kids in big cities.

"They're not just taking girls either," he continued. "I should clarify that. They're taking boys for various manual labor jobs and to work as future runners."

"I'm not sure I understand what you mean when you say 'runners,'" Maddie said.

"Runners basically do a little bit of everything," Nick supplied. "They're like assistants in weird ways. Sometimes they're in charge of repossessing cars when clients don't pay back gambling debts. Other times they do physical harm to get money from people who have secured loans and aren't paying them back."

"Like knee breakers?"

Nick nodded. "Exactly. Runners also serve as drivers when things need to be transported. A lot of the time it's drugs. That way if they're caught they only know the person ahead of them in the leader line and no one can touch the big dog."

"And Wally is the big dog?"

"I think we *thought* that Wally was the big dog," Dwight clarified. "We didn't know he had ties to bigger cities. I guess it's fair to say that Wally is the big dog in Detroit. He's on the second tier down from the biggest dogs, though, and apparently they jump from city to city."

"Is there one here in Detroit?" Nick asked.

"If you believe Wally there is," Dwight answered. "The thing is, we're in trouble when it comes to tracking this guy down. We've heard of him – whispers mostly – but he's pretty much a ghost."

"So you've heard of him but never tied him to Wally?" Maddie pressed. "How does that work?"

"Because no one has ever seen this guy," Dwight explained. "I'm not joking or exaggerating. Plenty of people have been picked up and tried to bargain deals of some sort and they often give the same name. El Capitan. We have no face or business address to associate with that name, though."

"He must be Hispanic," Nick argued. "I mean ... the name is Spanish."

"That's the prevailing theory, but we have no way to prove that and if we lock ourselves into that assumption we might miss something big," Dwight said. "What if it's merely a smart man who wants someone to believe we're dealing with a Hispanic individual?"

"Good point," Nick conceded. "So what do we know about this specific operation?"

"Wally says that the girls come to him from Chicago and he's supposed to sort through them," Dwight said. "The women who he thinks can fetch more money – the ones who have a bit of education and show an ability to learn – are moved to New York. Those who only have street value for drugs and prostitution are kept here and sometimes ferried over the bridge."

"And what happens on the other side of the bridge?" Maddie asked.

"I honestly don't know." Dwight wished he had better answers, but he couldn't give what he didn't have. "According to Wally other things happen in Canada and he doesn't have any information about what they're doing over there. I'm not sure I believe him, but he was adamant all the same."

"So what about the bodies?" Maddie asked the obvious question. "How do they play into this?"

"Wally swears up and down that he has nothing to do with the bodies. He thinks that someone wanted to take over his turf and planted the bodies there to take him down. If that's true, it would be an ingenious way to do it. I mean ... look how fast he's been taken out of commission."

"You don't seem as if you believe that," Nick pointed out. "How come?"

"Because those women were all killed in the same way and it doesn't feel like trafficking to me," Dwight replied. "It feels like a serial killer. Now, I'm not saying that a serial killer couldn't be a runner or vice versa. I can't quite wrap my head around those bodies belonging to one of Wally's cohorts, though."

"How come?" Maddie challenged.

"Because there's no money in dead women," Dwight replied. "Remember what I told you. These are businessmen. If they thought for a second they had a serial killer working for them they would handle it. Twenty women going missing in six months' time is something that would definitely send up an alert."

"But you said that the women are killed if they can no longer perform," Maddie argued. "How do we know that's not what's going on here?"

"I would be open to that suggestion if we only had one or two bodies," Dwight answered. "We have twenty, though. We also have more missing women. Some of the bodies belong to low-risk victims, which is something that the runners and Wally would never entangle themselves in because they don't want to make a mistake and take the wrong girl. If they did, that could mean huge news headlines.

"I mean, think about Natalee Holloway," he continued. "Now, granted, that was in Aruba and there were extenuating circumstances with that case, but what happens if we have a Natalee Holloway, Elizabeth Smart, or Jaycee Dugard situation here? That means a lot of attention on a small area and that is not what these guys want."

"I think I understand," Maddie mused, frustration evident on her pretty features. "You're basically saying you don't think Wally can lead us to a specific killer."

"I'm not entirely ruling it out," Dwight corrected. "I would be a lax detective to do that. I don't think I believe Wally had anything to do with the dead girls, though."

"So what do you want us to do?" Nick asked. "You clearly aren't getting the answers you want so you need Maddie to provide more."

"I want Maddie to do what she does best," Dwight replied. "I want her to feel things out on her own and follow her gut instincts. I need her to do it in a low-key fashion, though. I need her to be safe."

"That's why I'm here," Nick noted. "I won't let anything bad happen to her."

"I've never doubted that, son." Dwight offered up a weak smile. "Right now it feels as if we have two different cases. Those cases could eventually overlap, but we have to chase them as if they're separate."

"I understand." And, because she did, Maddie was more resolved than ever. "We'll walk around later and see if we can come up some leads. I don't know what else to do."

"Above all else, I want you to be safe," Dwight cautioned. "Don't put yourself at risk to get answers. Be careful. Be smart. Be safe. Those are your three biggest priorities."

"We'll do all of that," Maddie promised. "We'll find answers, too. I can't live with it if we don't."

That was exactly what Nick was afraid she would say.

10. TEN

With little to go on but the initial location, Maddie and Nick pointed themselves in that direction. Nick insisted Maddie head upstairs and change into muted colors and pull her hair back into a hat before leaving, though, and Maddie didn't bother to hide her agitation given his overbearing attitude as they walked down the street thirty minutes later.

"I think you're being ridiculous."

Nick expected her to put up a fight – if the roles were reversed and she was trying to tell him what to wear and how to act, there would definitely be an argument, after all – so he forced himself to remain calm. "I know you do. I'm sorry about that."

The apology wasn't enough to placate Maddie. "You forget that I spent six years of my life here."

"Oh, I could never forget that."

"I know the area," Maddie persisted. "I know how to talk to people on the streets. I talked to plenty of them when I worked at the hospital."

"I think this situation is a little bit different, Mad." Nick held out his arm to stop Maddie on the street corner as a light changed and traffic barreled past them. "You talked to people after they were injured. They were vulnerable. The people out here are going to be on the offensive. They want to make you feel vulnerable."

"Why do you think that?" Maddie was legitimately curious. "I would think the people out here would be happy to know that Wally is in jail and he's going to stay there for a bit. That makes the neighborhoods safer for them."

Nick bit back a sigh. She was so earnest at times it was grating. Usually he liked it – especially when they were in Blackstone Bay and the worst thing she had to worry about was how snarky Christy was going to be on any given day – but in a situation like this Nick felt Maddie's naiveté was a detriment.

"Yes, but now there will be a power vacuum and someone will try to fill it," Nick explained. "Wally was bad. No one would ever say otherwise. There's no way for the people who live here to know if the person who comes in next is going to be worse, though. That's going to be a big worry going forward."

"But ... maybe no one will come in."

This time Nick couldn't swallow his sigh. "You're so sweet and cute that I can't stand it." He leaned over and pressed a quick kiss to the corner of her mouth before they started walking again. "That's not the way the world works, though, Mad. Someone is going to come into this neighborhood and take over. It's simply the nature of the beast."

"Well, then I prefer a different beast."

Maddie and Nick held hands as they crossed the street, slowing their pace when they saw a group of police officers littering the lot. They had it completely shut off from anyone who might want to jump the fence, although their attention was on what looked to be an empty truck rather than the onlookers.

"There is another truck here," Maddie noted. "I wonder why."

"They're probably scouring it for evidence before transporting it to the impound lot," Nick said. "I'm guessing it belongs to Wally, too, so they had to search it. I think Dwight would've told us if more people were found, so it was probably empty. I doubt it will be here much longer either way."

"Still, it seems weird to me."

"Yeah, well ... where do you want to go first?" Nick wasn't keen on spending the afternoon downtown, especially since they were out in the open and he worried that news had spread about Maddie's involvement in the arrest. That's why he insisted on the hat. He was hopeful it would hide her flaxen hair, which would be a dead giveaway to those in the know.

"This way." Maddie tugged on Nick's hand and led him to a small alleyway between two buildings. The space was far enough away from the lot that they wouldn't draw attention from the gathered police officers.

"What are we doing here?" Nick asked, following Maddie into the alley.

"We have a guest in here," Maddie replied, smiling when she caught sight of Tina. The girl, who couldn't have been older than nine when she died, had pink barrettes in her hair and a quizzical look on her face. "How are you, Tina?"

Nick was used to listening to Maddie talk to air so he took up a protective stance at her side and continuously looked to both ends of the alley to make sure they wouldn't end up trapped. He figured Maddie would lead the conversation to the correct place because she had so much experience doing exactly that.

"It's busy today," Tina said, giving the appearance she was bouncing even though she didn't have physical feet to propel her along the sidewalk. "There are a lot of people here and Big Wally is gone. He hasn't been here all day."

"He's in jail," Maddie supplied. "He got himself in trouble yesterday and he's going to be in jail for five years."

Tina widened her eyes. "For real?"

Maddie nodded gravely. "For real. He's not coming back for a while."

"That's ... huh." Tina made a series of faces that Maddie found adorable. "I don't know what to think. I wish he was gone before because my brother was working for him when I got shot and I might still be alive if that happened."

Maddie's heart rolled. "I'm sorry about that. I really am. We can't go back in time, though."

"Oh, I know that." Tina was somber. "Even when it happens in books, that's not real. That's make believe ... like Santa and the Tooth Fairy."

"Yeah, well, it's still fun to imagine things like that." Maddie desperately wanted to touch the young girl and give her solace but it wasn't an option so she decided to focus on the business at hand. "What can you tell me about the people hanging around here today? Have they been saying anything?"

"I heard Old Mr. Jones say that we're never going to get any peace here now that all those bodies were found. He says the cops will move in and not leave until they've scared everyone off."

"Do you think that's true?"

Tina shrugged. "Mom can't leave because she doesn't have a lot of money so I don't think everyone will leave. Old Mr. Jones might leave, but it won't be everybody."

"No, probably not," Maddie agreed. "I see the police have a semi-trailer over across the way. Do you know if they found anything in it?"

"I was watching, but I went away for a little bit," Tina replied. "I missed when they opened it, but I think it was empty because the cops said it was a waste of time to come out here."

"I see." Maddie looked to Nick for help. "I don't know what to ask her."

"I think you're doing fine, love." Nick smiled. "I wish I could see Tina because she sounds delightful, but I think you're doing a good job getting your answers."

"He's pretty," Tina said wistfully, giggling as she took in Nick's tall frame. "He has pretty eyes and he looks pretty when he smiles at you."

"He's definitely pretty," Maddie agreed.

"Hey, are you guys talking about me?" Nick teased.

"Tina thinks you're pretty," Maddie volunteered. "I have to agree with her. You're the prettiest person I've ever seen in life."

Nick grinned. "Thank you. I feel the same way about you."

Maddie held Nick's gaze for a second longer than necessary before turning back to Tina. "Have you heard anything interesting today? We want to find the man who killed those girls, but we're not sure where to start."

"You should talk to Maraschino."

The simple statement caught Maddie off guard. "Who is Maraschino?"

"She's the woman over there." Tina pointed toward a bottle blond holding court on the corner across the street from the alley opening. She wore leather garters and a bustier that pushed her breasts up to fanciful heights. "She's not with no one so she might hear stuff from a bunch of different people."

"I don't know what that means," Maddie hedged. "She's not with anyone?"

"She's on her own."

"I ... ." Maddie broke off and ran her tongue over her lips. "Tina says we should talk to that woman Maraschino because she's not with anyone. I'm not sure what to make of that."

"I think she means Maraschino is an independent," Nick supplied. "She doesn't have a pimp and runs her own business. Since she's not loyal to any boss other than herself, she's more likely to take money in exchange for information."

"Oh." Maddie brightened. "That sounds like a great idea."

"Of course you would think that," Nick muttered under his breath.

"You don't think it's a good idea?" Maddie challenged. "May I ask why not?"

"I think it's a fabulous idea," Nick lied, allowing his sarcastic side to come out and play. "Let's go to the corner and talk to Maraschino, the famous independent prostitute. That's exactly how I saw this day going."

Maddie refused to let Nick drag her into an unnecessary fight. "I'm glad we're on the same page." She patted his hand. "Tina, we'll be around in case you want to talk later. We're going to talk to Maraschino now, though. Is she easy to get along with?"

Tina shrugged, seemingly unbothered about being abandoned. "She's probably not going to like you, but she's going to love him." Tina jerked a thumb in Nick's direction. "Have him do the talking."

Maddie wasn't sure that was going to be an option. "I'll keep that in mind."

NICK TRAILED BEHIND MADDIE as they crossed the street. He was alert, his eyes constantly scanning, but irritation threatened to overwhelm him and it took everything he had to keep from blowing up at Maddie. He couldn't believe how lackadaisical she was being in regards to her safety.

"Tina suggested you do the talking, but if you're not up for that I can do it," Maddie said as they hit the sidewalk.

Nick wrestled his full attention to his fiancée. "What?"

"Tina seemed to think that Maraschino would be more open to answering questions from you because you're a man. You're obviously annoyed, though, so if you don't think you can do it tell me now."

Nick scowled. "I think I can manage to ask a few questions."

"Great." Maddie's smile was impish. "I'm looking forward to watching you try. By the way, if she puts her hands on you I'm going to have to break them."

Even though he wasn't in the mood to question Maraschino, Nick couldn't stop himself from barking out a laugh. "I'm glad to know you're willing to fight for my honor."

Maddie gave Maraschino a cursory look as they approached. "I hope it doesn't come to that. I'm pretty sure she can take me."

"I think we'll be okay." Nick squeezed her hand. "Let me do the talking."

As it turned out, Nick didn't even have his mouth open before Maraschino decided she would be the one doing the talking.

"If you want a threesome that's going to cost you three figures," Maraschino warned, snapping her gum as she glanced between them. "It would've cost more if you were both ugly, but I can tell you both bathed today so I'll give you a deal."

"Oh, well, that's a very charming offer," Nick said, pulling a fifty from his wallet and holding it up. "As it happens, though, we're looking for information instead of calisthenics."

Maraschino rolled her eyes at the lame joke. "Of course you're looking for information, I should've seen that coming. You two clearly don't get adventurous when it comes to hitting the sheets."

Maddie couldn't stop herself from getting offended. "Hey! We're very adventurous."

"Don't let her get to you, Mad," Nick chided, flicking the fifty so it crackled. "Do you want the money or not?"

"I guess that depends on what answers you're looking for," Maraschino said after a beat. She very clearly wanted the money but she wasn't willing to answer questions until she knew the specifics of the agreement. "Are you looking for dirt on the cops or the criminals?"

It was an interesting question. "I guess we'll go with the criminals," Nick replied after a moment's hesitation. "We need to know what you can tell us about the bodies found in that lot."

"There isn't much to tell," Maraschino replied. "No one knew it was happening and when the bodies were discovered we were all shocked."

The response sounded rehearsed. "You had no idea it was happening?" Nick challenged. "How can that be? Are you telling me you never slipped into that lot to service a client?"

"I don't think I like the way you use the word 'service.'"

"How should I use it?"

"I don't know, but you're kind of judgmental," Maraschino argued. "The truth is, no one went to that lot because we all knew Big Wally owned it. No one wants trouble with Big Wally so we stay away. It was pretty simple."

"Obviously someone didn't stay away," Nick pressed.

"No, but that doesn't mean it has anything to do with Big Wally," Maraschino argued. "There's a rumor going around that all the women found in that field were independents and it was a warning from El Capitan that no one would be allowed to freelance on their own terms any longer."

Nick and Maddie exchanged a quick look.

"Have you ever met El Capitan?" Nick asked.

Maraschino shook her head. "No, and I don't want to. There's been a lot of pressure up and down the way for everyone to sign up with someone – at least for protection or something – but I don't want that. I want to be in charge of my own destiny."

"What will happen if El Capitan pushes the issue?" Maddie asked, forgetting that she was supposed to remain quiet. "Would he do something to you if you don't agree to his terms?"

"Oh, he'll definitely do something to me," Maraschino said. "It's not an if, it's a when."

"So what will you do?"

"Leave." Maraschino's answer was simple. "By the end of the week I will have enough to move my operation to Orlando. Personally, I can't wait to get out of here. I only have to hold on a bit longer."

"To your knowledge, did anyone see those bodies being dropped?" Nick asked. "I mean ... someone went into that lot at least twenty times to discard bodies. I can't say I buy the theory that they were all working girls – because I happen to know at least a few of them weren't – but even if the bulk were, someone had to carry those bodies into the lot. I have trouble believing that individual was never seen."

"That's because you don't understand the nature of this street," Maraschino said. "Everyone knows to be off the streets by two because otherwise it's bad news. That's when the runners are out, and you don't want to be out when they are. It will end up bad for anyone who wants to hide his or her face."

"Hmm." Nick stroked his chin. "What you're saying makes sense. The really bad stuff happens between two and five because that's when the police presence is at its lowest. The killer probably knew that and adjusted his plans accordingly. It would be much easier for him to operate at a time when no one was watching because the nature of street life made it dangerous for someone to look too hard."

"Exactly," Maraschino said, plucking the fifty from Nick's hand. "This is a rough area, but it's tolerable during the day. After midnight, it's a whole other world."

Nick nodded. "Thank you for the information. I hope you make it to Orlando safely."

"I do, too," Maraschino said. "It's just a few more days. I'm hopeful I'll be able to survive it."

"Why wouldn't you?" Maddie asked. "If you're an independent, why would someone want to stop you?"

"Because if word gets out that I manage to escape, it will be a source of hope for all those around me," Maraschino replied. "There's nothing more dangerous in the trenches than hope. Everyone knows that."

"You're definitely right." Nick grabbed another fifty from his wallet and handed it over. "Get out sooner rather than later if you can."

Maraschino accepted the bill. "Thank you. I'm definitely planning on it. In fact ... ." She trailed off at the sound of a car engine and flicked her eyes to a speeding vehicle as it raced around the corner.

Maddie had time to register two things before panic set in. The rear window of the car was down and there was a man with a gun poking his head out. That gun just so happened to be pointed in their direction. Everything else was a blur as time slowed down and she fought to force her body to move.

Nick realized their predicament at the same time and was spurred into action. "Get down!" he roared, throwing his body on top of Maddie's and pushing her toward the pavement.

The next thing Maddie heard was an explosion of bullets and all she could do was cover her ears and pray they would survive the assault. She was helpless otherwise.

11. ELEVEN

Maddie's heart pounded so hard the careening blood was enough to drown out the sounds of the gunfire as it set her veins on fire. Nick pressed her to the ground, completely covering her body with his, and she struggled to fight off the overwhelming shaking fit that overtook her. Ultimately she gave in, squeezed her eyes shut, and held on for dear life.

Maddie had no idea how long she was on the ground before Nick's voice finally penetrated the haze she willingly succumbed to.

"Maddie?"

She didn't immediately answer.

"Love, look at me!"

Maddie finally wrenched open her eyes, gasping when she found Nick's face two inches from hers. His eyes were wide and wild, worry etched across his handsome features. "Nicky."

"There you are," Nick choked out, exhaling heavily as he ran his hand over Maddie's torso. "Are you hurt? You didn't get hit, did you?"

"I ... ." Maddie mentally checked her body for points of pain. "I don't think so. My hip hurts a bit from hitting the pavement, but I'm okay."

"Are you sure?" It wasn't that Nick didn't believe her. It was simply that he needed to check himself. His heartbeat was slowly returning to normal, but just barely. He was almost manic as his hands searched Maddie's body. "What hurts? I don't care if you think it's minor. I want to know what hurts."

Maddie carefully pulled herself to a sitting position and rubbed her hand over her elbow. "I'm going to have a few bruises from hitting the ground, Nicky. I'm not hurt, though. In fact ... ." Something occurred to Maddie and she swiveled quickly to find Maraschino crouched low behind a Dumpster. The woman was as white as death, her chest heaving. Since her breasts were barely covered by her low-cut top, Maddie couldn't help but worry her impressive bosom would break free for the world to see, but that was hardly their biggest problem.

"Are you okay?" Maddie asked after a beat.

Maraschino shifted so her gaze snagged Maddie's. She looked shaken but determined. "I'm fine. I'm not the one who got hit."

"Who got hit?" Maddie asked, confused. "I'm okay. You're okay."

"Yeah, but your man isn't." Maraschino's tone was matter-of-fact. "Check out his shoulder. He's about to go down."

"What?" Maddie's eyebrows flew up her forehead as she turned and found Nick's normally healthy complexion going ashen. "Nicky?" She rolled up to her knees and searched his body for signs of trauma. Her gaze immediately fell on his left shoulder, the T-shirt material there torn as the blue fabric dampened with blood. "Oh, my ... Nicky."

Nick did his best to remain calm even though he sensed Maddie was going to fall apart. "I'm fine, Mad. It's just a graze." He grimaced as he attempted to rotate his shoulder. "It's not a bad wound."

Maddie wasn't about to take his word for it. She clawed at the shirt and ripped the shredded fabric away so she could get a better look, almost reeling back in shock at the sight of the blood. "Oh, Nicky." Maddie choked on the words. "I ... you ... ."

"Maddie!" Nick bellowed her name to get her to focus. She barely managed to lift her eyes and the way her lower lip trembled caused Nick's heart to constrict. "It's okay, Mad. I swear it's just a graze. It's not a bad wound. I'm not going to die on you or anything."

Maddie didn't appreciate his attempt at levity. "That's not funny."

"I know. We have to get off the street, though. We need to move into that alley and call Dwight."

Maddie stared at him for what felt like a very long time. In reality, it was probably only five seconds. "No, you need to go to the hospital."

"I'm not hurt that badly, Mad. That's not necessary."

"You're going to the hospital." Maddie was firm. She had to be. If she gave even an inch she would burst into tears and she didn't want Nick to feel as if he had to take care of her when he was nursing a gunshot wound. "Don't even think of arguing with me."

They were at a crossroads. Nick knew it. Compromise was in order and he was desperate enough to get her off the street that he had no problem agreeing to go to the hospital. "Fine," he conceded. "If you go in that alley until help arrives, I will go to the hospital. Then you will see my wound isn't that bad."

"As long as you're okay it doesn't matter."

Nick leaned over and gave her a quick kiss. "I swear I'm fine. Now ... help me get up. We need to call Dwight and get out of the line of fire."

ONCE DWIGHT AND THE ambulance arrived, Nick was more reticent about visiting the hospital. Maddie's courage found steady footing while waiting, though, and she was absolutely adamant about making sure Nick got proper medical care, so much so that she threatened to knock him out and carry him to the hospital herself if he didn't agree.

Ultimately Nick knew it would be quicker to go to the hospital than argue so he acquiesced.

"This isn't a bad wound," Dr. Tipton said as he flushed Nick's shoulder with fluids and prodded the tender flesh. "The bullet passed right through the skin and didn't hit any major arteries or blood vessels. It barely nicked you really. A couple of stitches and you'll be fine. You shouldn't even need pain medication, but if you want a couple doses I can write you a prescription."

Nick wasn't thrilled when he realized Tipton would be his doctor. He considered putting up a fight, but Maddie was so frazzled that adding to the insanity seemed like a poor idea so instead he accepted the doctor's haughty attention and fought the urge to punch him in the face every time Tipton looked at Maddie.

"I tried telling her that it wasn't a bad injury, but she didn't listen," Nick said. "She's a bit of a worrier."

"I don't think being upset about you getting shot makes me a worrier," Maddie fired back, combing her fingers through her messy hair. She removed the hat once they were in the ambulance and she'd been teasing out the snarls ever since. Nick was fairly certain it had nothing to do with vanity and everything to do with expending nervous energy.

"It's okay, love." Nick grabbed her hand with his good arm. "Come sit next to me. You're making me nervous with all the pacing you're doing."

Maddie did as he asked, rubbing her hand over his knee as she watched Tipton work. "You flushed out the area well, right? That alley was filthy and I don't want him getting an infection."

Tipton cocked a challenging eyebrow. "I believe I know how to clean out a wound, Ms. Graves."

Maddie didn't back down. "I'm just making sure. I'm kind of fond of him."

"So I've noticed," Tipton said dryly. "I was starting to wonder if you were a lesbian given your disinterest in men while you were here. I can see I was off the mark."

Nick furrowed his brow. "You thought she was a lesbian?"

Tipton shrugged, unbothered. "Why else would she turn me down? I mean ... it made no sense."

Nick could think of a million reasons Maddie might turn down Tipton. He was older than her, for a start. His personality reminded Nick of a rancid pickle. He never cracked a smile. There was something predatory about the way he looked at Maddie when he thought no one was watching. He was also full of himself and Nick was certain he had a god complex.

All of that added up to a self-important someone Nick had no intention of getting to know better.

"I think she had her mind on other things," Nick said easily, offering Maddie a charming smile as she rubbed her hand over his leg. "Mad, you need to take a breath. I'm okay. We'll be out of here in a few minutes so don't panic."

"I have a right to panic," Maddie muttered, shaking her head. "You almost died."

"Oh, geez." Nick pinched the bridge of his nose. "I didn't almost die. I was grazed. I'm perfectly fine."

"You shielded my body," Maddie groused. "You were almost killed protecting me."

Nick let loose with a long-suffering sigh as he tilted his head to the side and studied her. "Mad, I love you more than life itself. You know that, right?"

Maddie mutely nodded.

"Good." Nick's smile was tight-lipped. "You're driving me crazy. I didn't almost die. Of course I shielded you. It was instinct. Even if you weren't going to be my wife, though, I would've done the same for anyone else. That's what my training taught me."

"Well, I still don't like it." Maddie jutted out her lower lip, obstinate, and folded her arms across her chest. "I'm glad we live in Blackstone Bay. You're never almost shot when we're up there."

Nick didn't bother to hide his amusement. "No, I'm not," he agreed, chuckling. "However, you've almost drowned up there, a crazy person stalked you in your own garage, you were almost killed in a classroom at the school, you've been threatened by crazy ghost-hunting peeps, and you've had a few more run-ins as well. I almost prefer the city because you're in less danger."

Neither one of them believed that. Still, Maddie's expression softened as she leaned forward and rested her chin on Nick's chest. "You scared me."

"I'm sorry." Nick kissed her forehead. He understood the sentiment and overt worry. He'd felt it a time or two himself. "I didn't mean to frighten you. I simply reacted."

"I know. I'm just a little worked up. I can't help it."

"I'm okay with that." It was the truth. "I don't want you tying yourself into knots, though. I'm fine. You're fine. We're both fine."

"Yes. We're freaking lovely." Maddie made an exaggerated face and kissed the corner of his mouth before standing. "Dwight is in the hallway. While you're getting your arm sewed up, I'm going to see if he has any new information."

"I doubt he does."

"I need something to do."

Nick's nodded, understanding. "Okay. I'll be right here."

"Make sure you keep the stitches small and neat," Maddie ordered Tipton as she slid through the open doorway. "I don't want him to have too much of a scar. He's perfect the way he is."

"I'll see what I can do," Tipton said dryly, rolling his eyes as he watched Maddie stride into the hallway. "She's not the same as I remember her."

The statement caught Nick by surprise. "And how do you remember her?"

"She was a sweet and pretty girl who did what she was told and never caused waves," Tipton replied without hesitation. "She's not that woman any longer."

"She was never really that woman. At least she wasn't meant to be that woman. She didn't belong down here. She can be herself at home. That's where she belongs."

Tipton merely shrugged. "Some might think that living in a small town like Blackstone Bay is holding her back."

"And what do you know about Blackstone Bay?"

"Only what a map and Ms. Graves have told me, which admittedly isn't much. Still, there isn't a lot of opportunity up there for a woman with her skill set. You would think she would want to live close to a hospital so she could hone her skills."

Nick wanted to argue the point, but he wasn't sure he could. In truth, he and Maddie hadn't talked much about her degree and the fact that she wasn't using it in Blackstone Bay. He made a mental note to bring it up once they got home. If Maddie wanted to be a nurse there were hospitals that weren't overly far and they could make it work. He wanted to kick himself for not bringing it up sooner.

"Maddie can make her own decisions."

"I'm sure she can," Tipton said. "I'm going to send in a nurse to prepare the area for stitches and I will be back in ten minutes. It shouldn't take long and then we'll have you out of here."

"I'm looking forward to that."

Nick wasn't alone two minutes before a striking brunette woman in blue scrubs breezed her way into the room. She had a bright smile on her face as she snapped a pair of rubber gloves into place.

"You must be Nick Winters. You're the talk of the floor."

Nick didn't know what to make of that. "Um ... ."

"I'm Andrea Hopper," the woman introduced herself. "I used to work with Maddie when she was here. I always liked her and was sad when she left, but now I see she was running toward something rather than away from this place and the creeps who work here."

Nick was even more confused than when the woman started talking. "I don't know what you mean. Did you think Maddie was running away from something?" He did his level best to relax as Andrea poked at the wound on his arm.

"I considered it for a bit," Andrea replied. "Maddie was upset one of the last times I saw her. Tipton and Bishop were practically drooling over her as they battled for her affection. Most women would get off on something like that, but Maddie isn't most women. Although, I guess you know that."

Andrea offered up a hollow laugh before shaking her head. "Anyway, Maddie was uncomfortable with them constantly asking her out. They're doctors so they think they're the biggest dudes on the planet and everyone should bow down to them. Because Maddie wouldn't, because she said over and over that she wasn't interested, that made them all the more interested when she refused to go out with them."

Nick was slowly catching on, although he still felt there were a few gaps to fill. "Who is Bishop?"

"Oh, Dr. Phillip Bishop," Andrea answered, smirking. "I forgot you're not part of the in-crowd. He's the chief of internal medicine here and he was absolutely in love with Maddie from the moment he saw her. I swear I saw him drooling a few times."

Nick found himself caught in an odd predicament. He felt bad for talking about Maddie behind her back – although his attention was focused on those who chased her more than anything else – but he was also getting insight that he couldn't very well tune out.

"So basically you're saying every doctor in this hospital went after Maddie and she turned them down, huh?"

"I think she turned most of them down," Andrea clarified. "I seem to remember her going out on a date or two – although not with either of those clowns – and she was unhappy when she came back. I didn't understand it at the time because I would love to bag a doctor. Heck, that's half the reason I became a nurse."

"Yes, I can see that," Nick said dryly.

"That wasn't why Maddie was here, though," Andrea supplied. "I often wondered if she knew why she was here. She liked helping people, don't get me wrong, but life seemed to be dragging her down toward the end. I wasn't surprised when I heard she was leaving."

"You weren't?" Nick was intrigued. "Everyone else I've run into seemed surprised that she would even want to leave."

"That's probably because she was so well respected here," Andrea explained. "She was one of the few people who never caused problems or engaged in extended rounds of gossip. She wasn't interested in screwing around with doctors or anything. In fact, most of the time when I talked to her, she seemed lonely, as if she were yearning for something."

Nick's heart pinged. "Oh."

Andrea's face filled with a bright smile as she lifted her eyes. "I see now what she was yearning for."

"I don't think she came home for me," Nick hedged, although even as he said the words he realized they probably weren't true. "She didn't come home *only* for me," he corrected quickly. "She came home because Blackstone Bay is where she belongs."

"I believe that." Andrea beamed. "Maddie never looked as happy when she was living down here as she does now. Even though she's upset about you getting shot, you can see she has a glow about her. She was even forceful when Bishop asked her out for coffee in the hallway."

Nick's shoulders jerked at the news, causing Andrea to lift an eyebrow.

"I can see you didn't know that," Andrea said after a beat. "Just for the record, there's a reason why no one here confides in me. I have an absolutely huge mouth. I know better and yet I can't stop myself from saying the wrong thing at the exact worst moment."

"I happen to find that refreshing." Nick opted for honesty. "I am concerned, though. You said that this Dr. Bishop asked Maddie out for coffee. When was that?"

"I heard him when I was coming in," Andrea replied. "Maddie was talking to that detective she used to hang around with – come to think of it, everyone was convinced she was having an affair with him, too, but I'm guessing that wasn't true – when Dr. Bishop approached and asked her to catch up over coffee.

"Maddie was very polite – she's always that way, after all – but said she was going to be with you all day and then thanked him for the invitation," she continued. "I could tell Bishop was bothered by it, but he didn't seem to be throwing a fit or anything, and just between you and me, that dude is not above throwing a fit."

"Can you point him out to me?" Nick had no idea why he was so interested in seeing the man for himself, but he couldn't stop the agitation and unease from growing in his belly. "I just want to know what my competition looks like."

"Oh, honey, you don't have any competition," Andrea drawled. "You're hotter than all the doctors in this place put together. Still, I get why you want to know. Lean to your right."

Nick did as instructed and stared into the hallway. The first thing he saw was Maddie talking to Dwight, her hands flying to and fro as she reenacted what happened on the street corner. She seemed oblivious to anything and anyone else. Behind her, though, a man stood in his white physician's coat, hands in his pockets. He stared hard at Maddie, his gaze never moving from the animated blond.

"It's him."

Nick already knew who Andrea was going to point toward before she did it. "I see. He looks older. How come he isn't married?"

"He wants to sample every ice cream flavor on the menu before that happens," Andrea replied. "I think the only flavor he's interested in that he hasn't been able to taste is Maddie ... and it doesn't sit well with him."

That little tidbit only made Nick feel worse. "Let's get moving on my arm. I don't want to be here longer than I have to be."

"I don't blame you in the least for that. Let's get it done."

12. TWELVE

"Stop fussing."

Nick was agitated, although he couldn't figure out why. After their trip to the hospital, Maddie insisted on returning to the hotel so he could rest. Even though he wasn't a fan of being infantilized, Nick agreed to her suggestion because he wanted her out of the hospital and away from her testosterone-fueled fan club.

In his head, Nick knew that dwelling on the fact that two doctors asked Maddie out during a time when they weren't together was ridiculous. He couldn't shake his unease, though, and he was starting to take it out on Maddie.

"I said to knock it off." Nick slapped at Maddie's hands as she checked the bandage on his arm. They were heading to dinner – set to meet Dwight and Sage for a meal at one of the Renaissance Center's most popular restaurants – and he was hopeful his agitation was merely a symptom of being hungry. Otherwise he had no explanation, which made him feel guilty. That guilt was manifesting via a bout of snark, though, and he couldn't seem to control himself.

Maddie widened her eyes to saucer-like proportions. "I didn't mean to hurt you."

"You didn't hurt me. I'm not in pain. I simply don't like it when you fuss over me."

"I ... well ... okay." Maddie turned to grab her keycard from the table so they could exit their room. "I'm sorry."

Nick didn't miss the look on her face. She was fighting her own bout of annoyance. Another emotion crowded her beautiful features as well, though, and that was hurt. "No, Mad, I'm sorry." Nick felt like a jerk. "I didn't mean to snap at you. It's been a long day."

"It has," Maddie agreed, keeping her gaze averted. "You should get some red meat with your dinner. You need the iron and protein."

Nick pursed his lips. "I believe it was you giving me grief about eating too much red meat two weeks ago, if I'm not mistaken."

"You should have it tonight. It always puts you in a good mood." Maddie reached for the door handle. "Are you ready? It won't take us long to get to the restaurant, but we have to do a bit of walking."

"I'm ready." Nick snagged Maddie's hand as she moved to walk through the doorway. "I'm sorry, love. I shouldn't be taking this out on you."

Maddie opened her mouth but seemingly thought better about what she was going to say and changed course. "You've had a long day. You got shot."

"I didn't get shot. I was grazed."

"With a bullet. That's the same as being shot."

"I think we'll simply have to agree to disagree there." Nick heaved out a sigh as he watched the room door drift shut. He tested it to make sure it latched and then linked his fingers with Maddie's as they walked down the hallway. "I really am sorry about snapping at you. I didn't mean it."

"I know you didn't." Maddie put on a brave face and forced a smile. "It's fine. When you get shot, you get to snap as much as you want. That's the rule."

Nick hated that she was making excuses for him. "I'm done snapping at you."

"Okay. Still, I think you should have some red meat. That always brightens your mood."

Nick understood what she wasn't saying. He was making her unhappy with his attitude, and that's the last thing he wanted. "I definitely will be getting red meat." Nick squeezed her hand. "I'm going all out for dinner tonight. I want you to do the same."

"I haven't eaten since breakfast," Maddie admitted, causing Nick to furrow his brow. "I wasn't sure if I was hungry but now, all of a sudden, I'm ravenous."

Nick searched his memory and realized he'd eaten a sandwich at the hospital but Maddie, who had been all nerves and fluttery energy, ignored the one Andrea brought for her to munch on. "You really haven't eaten for hours, have you?"

"I'm fine," Maddie said hurriedly. "I couldn't have eaten when I was worried about you anyway."

"Well, you're eating an entire cow by yourself tonight. I think we can arrange for some mushrooms and onions to join the party as well. Oh, and dessert. You're going to eat your weight in cake."

Maddie giggled at the visual, the sound loosening some of the tension solidifying around Nick's heart. "That sounds like a plan."

They lapsed into amiable silence, the weight of the day lifting as they exited the elevator and walked across the courtyard. Nick was the first to speak.

"Do you know where you're going?"

Maddie nodded. "It's an absolutely fabulous chophouse. It's right around the corner."

"That's convenient."

"I only ate here once when I lived down here, but it was really good. If you can't find a steak here that will make you happy, I think we're in for a rough night."

Nick slowed his pace and drew Maddie to him. "I'm sorry for snapping at you. I really am."

"It's okay. It's my fault you got shot."

Nick balked. "It most certainly is not!"

"I wanted to go down there. You positioned yourself to protect me. It is my fault."

"No, it's not, Maddie." Nick was at his limit. "Love, I went down there because we needed answers. I protected you because that's what instinct told me to do. You are not to blame for this."

Maddie didn't look convinced. "We'll make sure you get a good night's sleep tonight." She patted his arm. "I'll take care of you."

"Oh, geez." Nick rubbed his free hand across his forehead. "You're going to be a pain all night. I can already tell. You're definitely eating your weight in cake because sugar makes you happy."

"I guess we'll be a happy couple then, huh?"

Nick nodded without hesitation as they started walking. "Definitely."

DWIGHT AND SAGE WERE already seated at a cozy table in the corner when Maddie and Nick arrived. Sage bounced to her feet and immediately threw her arms around Maddie's neck, causing Maddie to have to plant her feet to stay upright.

"I'm so glad you're finally here," Sage enthused.

"Yes, I thought Sage was going to pass out from the anticipation," Dwight said dryly.

Nick smiled at the girl when she turned her attention to him and offered her a mild hug as Sage grinned like a loon. "You look good, Sage. It's really good to see you."

"Of course I look good." Sage smoothed the front of her peasant blouse as she stood back. "The last time you saw me I'd been held captive for days. Anyone would look rough after an ordeal like that."

"Definitely," Nick agreed, holding out Maddie's chair so she could sit. "How are you doing otherwise?"

"Great." Sage seemed obscenely happy. "School is going well and I'm caught up from the time I missed. I'm in a new dorm room and I like the girls on my floor a lot. Oh, and I'm dating someone."

The last part caught Maddie off guard. "Really?" She grinned. "That sounds great. You'll have to tell me all about it."

"Yes, I love hearing talk about the boyfriend," Dwight drawled, rolling his eyes as he sipped a beer. "I can't tell you how excited I am that Sage has found a serious boyfriend. It doesn't bother me in the slightest."

Nick smirked. "That sounded very well-rehearsed."

"Yeah, yeah." Dwight waved off the comment. "Sage is happy so I'm happy."

"Have you met the boyfriend yet?"

Dwight shook his head. "Apparently he's afraid to meet me. Personally, I think that's a point in his favor."

Nick snorted out a laugh. "Ah, I can already tell this relationship is going to be fun."

"You need to tell me about him," Maddie prodded. "I want to know everything."

Sage's eyes sparkled. "Okay, but we should probably do it in the bathroom because Dad says he's sick of hearing about him."

"Oh, I'm sure he doesn't mean that."

"No, I mean it." Dwight made small shooing motions to get Maddie and Sage to depart. "If you're going to talk about Corey – that's his name, by the way, although I'm not sure if that's a man or woman's name quite frankly – then you should do it elsewhere."

Sage rolled her eyes. "We'll do it in the bathroom. I don't want to hear his comments a second time anyway. I have photos for you though, Maddie."

"That sounds great." Maddie cast Nick a quick look as she stood. "Can you order for me?"

Nick nodded. "Porterhouse?"

"And mashed potatoes and whatever else you think I might like. I really am starving."

"That's what happens when you skip lunch." Nick watched her go, his lips curving when Sage leaned close to Maddie and whispered something that made both women giggle. When he turned back to Dwight, he found the detective watching him with a speculative look. "What?"

"How are you feeling?"

Nick groaned. "Oh, not you, too. I'm perfectly fine. It was barely a scratch. I wouldn't have even gotten the stitches if Maddie wouldn't have made such a fuss about it."

"Not that." Dwight rolled his neck. "I meant the other thing. It was very clear you were agitated in the hospital this afternoon, and I have a feeling I know why."

Nick played with the condensation ring left behind by his water glass as he shifted in his chair. "I don't know what you're talking about."

"You're a terrible liar." Dwight made a clucking sound with his tongue. "I saw the look on your face when you were watching Maddie. You were agitated by Dr. Bishop."

Nick considered lying, but since Dwight was the only friend he had in the area he opted to go the other way. "Will you think less of me as a man if I admit that I don't like the way that any of those doctors look at Maddie?"

"No."

"Well, I hate it." Nick felt like a pathetic jerk. "I don't know what I was thinking. I mean ... I've always known she was beautiful. When she left Blackstone Bay, I think part of me wanted to pretend she would turn ugly or something because I didn't want to think about it. If I spent too much time pondering the truth, it would've driven me insane."

"I think you and Maddie are unique in a lot of ways." Dwight chose his words carefully. "You guys fell in love as children, but you separated at a time when you were both exploring and debating who you were going to become as adults. Honestly, I think that was the best time for you to separate. It allowed you to be fully formed individuals when you got your second chance."

"I believe that wholeheartedly," Nick said. "I've never really given what Maddie did down here too much thought because it bothered me to think about her being alone. Now, though, I've found that the idea of her not being alone – the mere notion of those jerks hitting on her – has twisted me up in a way I didn't think was possible."

"You're jealous."

"I don't like that word."

"That doesn't mean it's not the right word." Dwight took another long swig of his beer before continuing. "I get it. Up until now it's been pretty obvious that Maddie has only ever had eyes for you.

Seeing the way the doctors in that hospital follow her around like trained puppy dogs has to be annoying."

"It is annoying," Nick agreed. "Worse, though, I've snapped at her three or four times this afternoon because I was annoyed with the doctors, not her. I never snap at her."

"I know. You're usually the puppy dog when it's just you and Maddie." Dwight grinned at Nick's scowl. "I'm messing with you, man. As for the doctors, you should know that even when Maddie was down here before, she didn't show them any interest. I didn't know about you at the time, but I always thought she was searching for something. I didn't know what that something was, but I was hopeful she would find it.

"Then, one day not long after she left, I got a call from you," he continued. "You sounded so concerned, so worked up, that I realized she'd found what she was looking for. I also realized you two didn't quite realize how important you would end up being to each other ... at least not yet. Thankfully for all of us you put things together fairly quickly. By the time I visited you guys, it was obvious she was exactly where she was supposed to be."

"I don't know if you're just saying that to make me feel better, but I'll take it." Nick sipped his water. "The thing is, I don't like being jealous. I know those doctors didn't mean anything to her, but I feel territorial whenever anyone looks at her the way I do."

"Son, you're the only one who can look at her the way you do. Do you want to know why? Because she looks back. She's never looked at anyone but you as far as I can tell."

"I like to tell myself that, but she's clearly been involved with other people over the years. She wasn't a virgin our first time together."

"Ugh." Dwight slapped his hand to his forehead. "Did you have to tell me that?"

"I'm sorry." Nick held up his hands in a placating manner. "I didn't mean to gross you out. I've just been forced to face some deep thoughts that I would rather not have to be facing and apparently I've turned myself into a grouch."

"I don't think that's true," Dwight countered. "You had other things going on. You were almost shot – we're still investigating that, by the way, and we don't think it has anything to do with the bodies at this point – and Maddie is convinced you were actually shot. That's been grating on you. She turned herself into Florence Nightingale to dote on you, which you should just let her do because she has a nurturing manner and she needs it.

"You saw two guys hitting on her, which irritates the crap right out of you," he continued. "That's on top of the fact that you keep thinking about what might have been, and I'm not talking about what might have been if you hadn't moved fast enough to put her on the ground when you first heard those shots.

"Don't get me wrong, you've been entertaining thoughts about that, too," he said. "I think your biggest problem is that this trip has made you confront the idea that things might not have turned out so well for you if Maddie never came home. And, while it's none of my business, I think the bigger part of you is mad at yourself because you didn't come down here to collect her sooner."

Nick touched the tip of his tongue to his top lip as he considered the statement. "How did you know I was thinking that?"

"Because it's what I would be thinking in your shoes. I don't know that I've ever believed in fate and destiny, but I know I definitely didn't believe in those concepts before I saw you and Maddie together. If any two people ever belonged together, it's you."

"I have been whipping myself about that," Nick admitted ruefully. "I hate knowing we missed time together. Some of that time was necessary. Not all of it was, though. I should've come for her years ago. Even when I was trying to delude myself that I hated her I knew that I still loved her."

"And she knew it, too, which is why she came home," Dwight said. "Her mother's death might have been the catalyst, but you were the reward and she's finally come to the realization that she deserves her reward."

"That's a very sweet thing to say," Nick teased, hoping to lighten the moment. "I had no idea you felt that way about me."

"Oh, I don't." Dwight was droll. "To me, you're the same as that Corey who wants to romance my daughter. You're both filthy animals."

"Good to know."

Dwight's eyes twinkled. "The thing is, Nick, you've got to accept the fact that you've already won. Being jealous and trying to smother Maddie with affection – and even protection – while you're down here isn't going to help. It's only going to hurt.

"She needs to feel the freedom she did when she lived down here to reinforce that she's where she's supposed to be," he continued. "She's a pragmatic soul and she's good at what she does. She'll never love anyone but you. So, my question is, what exactly are you worried about?"

Nick searched his mind for an answer and came up empty. "I want her safe," he offered lamely.

"I know. You can't watch her every moment of every day, though. Give her a little breathing room. You've been snapping at her all day and you don't like it. Maybe that's a hint that you need a little breathing room, too."

Nick pursed his lips as he nodded. "I'll give it some thought."

"That's all I ask."

13. THIRTEEN

Nick and Maddie were back on track the next morning, or at least as close as they could get while living in a hotel room. The dinner lasted long into the evening, laughter and jokes flying fast and furious. When they returned to their room, Nick allowed Maddie to play nurse for him and the game turned romantic. When they both woke, they were entwined around one another and happy.

"I could eat an entire truckload of bacon," Nick announced as they headed into one of the Renaissance Center's diners. "I don't understand why I'm so hungry after the pile of food I ate last night."

Maddie cocked a flirty eyebrow. "Oh, that hurts my feelings. I thought you were going to blame me for your appetite."

Nick grinned. "I'm always hungry for you." He gave her a quick kiss before settling across the booth from her. "So, other than eating a big breakfast, what are your plans for the day?"

The way he phrased the question caught Maddie off guard. "I'm not sure. I haven't given it a lot of thought yet. I was thinking I would stop by the hospital and check in with the girls."

"Okay." Nick's answer was easy, too easy for Maddie to swallow.

"You're not going to fight me on that?" she challenged.

"Should I fight you on that?"

"Well, no, but ... you've been fighting me on a lot of stuff the last few days and I thought for sure you would give me grief about it."

Nick thought back to his conversation with Dwight the night before. The man had been married for more than twenty years and he and his wife were still happy. That was the sort of relationship Nick wanted with Maddie so he gave serious consideration to Dwight's words.

"I was a jerk yesterday." Nick was matter-of-fact. "I shouldn't have acted the way I did. I don't have much of a defense, but I promised to always be straight with you and, honestly, my nose was a little out of joint."

"Why?"

"Because every doctor at that hospital was apparently in love with you and it bothered me to watch them follow you around, their tongues practically hanging out of their mouths. I don't like admitting I was jealous, but I was."

"You were jealous?" Maddie was flabbergasted. "Why? You're the only person I've ever wanted."

Nick smiled, warmth washing over him. "I know. I was being a weirdo. I can't explain it. I'm truly sorry, though. It was me, not you. None of what happened is on you, and if I made you feel that, the fault is with me and you'll never know how sorry I am."

Maddie tapped her bottom lip as she regarded him. Her eyes were serious, but Nick sensed a hint of playfulness lurking beneath her stern exterior. "I'm sorry, too."

"Why are you sorry?"

"For being so irresistible you couldn't hold back your jealousy."

Nick let loose with a hearty guffaw. "Ha, ha." He gripped her fingers tightly on top of the table for a beat and then relaxed. "I think it's probably a good idea for you to head to the hospital alone. I don't do well with all your male fans, and I get the feeling you might enjoy having lunch with some of the other nurses so you can catch up on gossip."

"I don't gossip."

"All women gossip. It's fine. I'm pretty sure your friends are going to want to gossip about me – because I'm irresistible, too – and this will give you a chance to talk freely without worrying about entertaining me."

Maddie welcomed the offer, but she remained conflicted. "Are you sure? What are you going to do?"

"I'm going to go through some missing person files with Dwight," Nick replied, not missing a beat. "He mentioned needing help yesterday and I volunteered. We're trying to match faces with names. Once we have a smaller list, we're hoping you can look through the files and tell us if any of the women were the ones you saw in your vision."

"Oh." Maddie was mollified. "That sounds like a good idea."

"It does," Nick agreed. "Just promise me to text when you're leaving the hospital so I know to look for you."

"The hospital is only two blocks from the police station," Maddie reminded him. "I made that walk at least a hundred times when I lived here and nothing ever happened."

"Yes, well, I'm hopelessly devoted to my irresistible girl and I want to know." Nick kept his tone playful but didn't back down. "That will be our compromise for the day."

"I think it's a good compromise."

"I wholeheartedly agree. Now, let's eat. I'm going to need a full stomach if I hope to make it through the morning without worrying."

MADDIE WAS IN A GOOD mood when she hit the hospital. Nick seemed more like his usual self and she couldn't help being giddy knowing that she was returning to the facility under her own free will rather than being forced to walk through the front doors, which was exactly how she felt the last few years of her tenure. It was a slog each and every day she returned, but now it felt voluntary and she appreciated that.

She was almost to the front steps when a familiar figure stepped out from under the eave and cut off her avenue of approach.

"I'm so glad you're alone," Sage said, causing Maddie to rear back and gasp. "Dad said Nick was going to be helping him and you were going to be doing something else for a few hours and I took a chance that you were coming here."

"You scared the crap out of me, Sage," Maddie complained, slapping at the girl's hand. "What are you doing here?"

"I was going to call you and ask you to come to me, but I didn't want to take a chance."

"The chance to what?"

"I might know something about Dad's case," Sage hedged, averting her gaze.

Maddie's heart tripped at the admission. "I'm sorry but ... what? You know something about a serial killer and you haven't told your father about it. What are you thinking?"

"I don't know anything about a serial killer," Sage clarified. "At least ... I'm not sure if I do. I happen to know some people laying low, though, and I've been helping them a little bit by dropping off food while I'm home."

Maddie was utterly confused. "I don't understand what you're saying, Sage. What exactly do you know?"

"I think it's better if I show you," Sage replied. "It's close. It's a safe place – at least for us – and it's really not far. I think you need to see it to understand."

Maddie licked her lips as she regarded the hospital's front doors. "I promised Nick I would be here all morning before joining him at the police station. I didn't mention anything about going on an adventure with you."

"It's not really an adventure. It's more of a mercy mission than anything else. I thought you would be up for that."

Maddie made a face. "You know exactly where to hit me, don't you?"

Sage shrugged, noncommittal. "You risked your life to save me. You don't have to risk your life to help the people I'm going to introduce you to, but it's a weird situation. I honestly thought you would want to help."

Maddie made a tsking sound as she shook her head. "That

was low."

"I didn't know where else to go." Sage's expression was plaintive. "I think that your case and my people may overlap, but I'm not sure how and I'm terrified to talk to my father because he won't understand what I've been doing."

Maddie didn't want to involve herself in Dwight's relationship with his daughter, but she recognized the desperation on Sage's face. "Okay. Show me what you've got. If this is bad, though, I'm going to call Dwight myself."

"Do you have to?"

"I won't make a promise otherwise. I want to do what's right for you and I can't make that decision until I see."

"Well, what you're going to see has very little to do with me and very much to do with fear. I think you'll want to keep this secret when you see what's going on. It's ... well, it's out of this world."

"OH, I'M GOING TO KILL YOU."

Maddie's eyes were so wide as she glanced around the dilapidated main floor of an abandoned library ten minutes later that Sage was convinced the woman's blue orbs might pop right out of her head.

"It's not so bad," Sage argued, wringing her hands as she stood in what used to be the library's main foyer. "It's a community of sorts."

It was a community all right. It was a community of high-risk individuals hiding out in a building that looked as if it was one stiff breeze away from crumbling inward. There was no furniture or books, just empty shelves and people huddling in various corners.

Maddie took stock of the situation relatively quickly, counting heads and searching faces. She estimated that about fifty people were hiding in the building – and that was only the main floor, for all she knew another fifty could be on the second floor – and all of them looked ragged and a little worse for wear.

"What is this, Sage?"

"They're women of the street," Sage explained. "They've built a community to protect themselves because word is out about a predator. When I first heard them talking, I thought they were exaggerating the threat. Then my dad was called in on the case and well ... now I'm not so sure they were exaggerating."

"Sage, I can't believe you hid this from your father." Maddie threw up her hands, furious. "He would want to help. These girls need help." As if to prove her point, Maddie moved closer to a young Hispanic-looking girl cowering against a bookshelf. She knelt down and offered up a soft smile. "Hi. I'm Maddie. Are you okay? Do you need something?"

The girl didn't answer, instead covering her mouth with a pair of filthy hands.

"She can't speak English," Sage offered. "She's here illegally."

That's when things clicked into place for Maddie. She swiveled slowly, taking a moment to study each visible face a second time. "They're all here illegally, aren't they?"

"Most," Sage acknowledged. "Some of them are runaways."

"Underage runaways?"

"Well ... ." Sage sucked in a breath. "The runaways here didn't come because they were spoiled and sick of rules at home. Most of them were being mistreated – some were being sexually abused – and this was a better escape for them."

"A better escape?" Maddie was understandably dubious. "Sage, these girls are living in a building without heat and running water. They're at the mercy of whoever finds them. What happens if a bad person finds this building and decides to take them? There's no recourse. No one will even know they're gone to report them missing."

"I can't fix that," Sage said earnestly. "That's above my paygrade. I can bring them food and drinks so they don't go hungry and thirsty, though. That's the best I can do."

"And what do you want me to do?"

"Talk to them. You know more about the case than I do. Dad doesn't like to bring his work home with him. I think some of these people might know who you're dealing with."

"Really?" Maddie scratched the back of her neck. The building was so dark and dank she was convinced spiders were dropping from the ceiling into her hair. "Point me toward someone who might have answers."

"Very few of them speak English," Sage said, wrapping her fingers around Maddie's wrist to direct her toward an alcove in the adjacent room. "Mercedes speaks well, though, and she knows a little bit about everything."

"Great. I can't wait to meet her."

IT TURNED OUT MERCEDES – no last name because the woman didn't trust Maddie enough to share it – really was easy to understand. She was a no-nonsense woman in her thirties and she seemed frustrated with Sage for giving up their hiding place.

"I knew you were going to be trouble," Mercedes muttered, wrinkling her nose. "The minute you walked through the door with your basket of groceries and pile of questions I knew you were going to make things more difficult for us."

"That's not my intention," Sage argued. "It's just ... you were telling that story last week and I wasn't sure if I believed it. Then it turns out that my father is on a case where a bunch of bodies were discovered in a lot down the way. Now Maddie is in town, which means things are serious. I need you to tell her what you told me."

Mercedes eyed Maddie with cool detachment. "And what is it that you offer to help this ... problem?"

Maddie returned the woman's even gaze. "I have a certain ability that might play a factor. More importantly, I want to help. What happened in that lot is not acceptable. I want to make sure it never happens again."

"So you're a crusader?"

"I wish the world were a better place," Maddie clarified. "I can only do what I can do, though. I don't think I'm omnipotent or all-powerful."

"Yes, well ... ." Mercedes thoughtfully rubbed her hand over her chin as she regarded Maddie with unreadable eyes. "One of the girls who lives here says that someone freed a truck of potential slaves two days ago. She was watching as it happened and said a woman with the prettiest yellow hair she'd ever seen tipped off the cops."

Since Mercedes didn't ask a question, Maddie remained silent.

"That was Maddie," Sage said quickly. "She's the one who saved those women. She's been visiting them in the hospital, too. She's a good woman."

"I believe the person who saved our brethren from the back of that trailer had good intentions," Mercedes said. "The problem is, all those women will now be deported and lose their one and only shot of making the United States their home. I'm not sure if that makes things better or worse for our people."

"I can't change that." Maddie refused to apologize for a scenario she couldn't correct. "I'm not with the state department or immigration services. I'm a small-town woman who used to work as a nurse a few blocks over."

"A nurse, huh?" Mercedes didn't look impressed. "And what do you do now?"

"I own a magic shop in northern Lower Michigan."

"A magic shop?"

Maddie nodded.

"So you think you're magic, huh?"

"Maddie *is* magic," Sage said hurriedly, clearly nervous due to the way the two women eyed each other. "She's psychic. She found me when I was missing and everyone already thought I was dead."

Maddie let loose with an exasperated sigh. "Sage, have you ever thought about shutting your mouth before you say the exact wrong thing?"

Sage's face was blank. "What did I say?"

Maddie rolled her eyes and waved off the question. "It doesn't matter. What does matter is the women here and the situation you find yourselves in. This isn't a safe environment."

"It's much safer than what's out there," Mercedes argued.

"And what's out there?"

"A monster."

Maddie pretty much expected the answer, but she needed more information before she could proceed. "Is it the same monster who locked up those girls in the truck?"

"That's an interesting question. Most people assume we're dealing with the same monster. You don't seem to believe that, though."

"Honestly? I assumed that to be the case from the start, but then two people I happen to respect a great deal explained things to me. It makes no sense for the type of monster who makes money selling girls into sexual slavery to kill them off before making a profit. That means we're dealing with a second type of monster."

"We are," Mercedes agreed. "It's even more insidious than you imagine, though, because the monster you're looking for wears the face of an angel."

Maddie had no idea what to make of that. "I ... um ... what do you mean?"

"He wears one face for the public and hides the other until he can unveil it to us," Mercedes explained. "He pretends to be a good man even as evil runs through his veins. Most people call him a saint, but we know him as a sinner."

Maddie wasn't big on religious symbolism so she struggled to understand Mercedes' words. "Do you know who killed those girls? Do you know who we're looking for?"

Mercedes shook her head. "I don't have a name, but I do know he's a man who pretends to help others."

"How?"

"One of our girls managed to escape from the monster, but only after he pretended to be a strong man," Mercedes explained. "She barely escaped with her life and now she remains traumatized."

"Okay. Who are we dealing with?"

"I don't know the name or the face, but I do know the profession. He's a doctor ... at the very hospital that sits less than a mile down the road."

All the oxygen in Maddie's lungs whooshed out. "Are you sure?"

"Positive."

Maddie looked to Sage, dumbfounded. "Well ... crap."

14. FOURTEEN

Maddie knew Nick would be furious so she called Dwight. Technically she was following the chain of command. Er, well, that was the way she rationalized it. She was a mess, though, as she stood at the front of the building and waited for the two men to arrive.

Nick was a picture of bridled fury when he exited Dwight's vehicle. Maddie could practically feel the rage radiating from him.

"I'm sorry about all this," Maddie offered apologetically. "I didn't know who else to call."

Dwight flashed her a wan smile. "You did the right thing. Where is my daughter?"

Maddie didn't like the way he said "my daughter," but she plastered a smile on her face all the same. "She's inside. She's angry at me for calling you. I didn't see where we had a lot of options, though. I wanted to question the girl who claims she was attacked but managed to escape, but I knew that was a bad idea and could inadvertently taint the investigation."

"There's been some back and forth for the last hour," she continued. "Sage is upset because she feels I betrayed her. Mercedes – she's the woman who runs things here – is convinced I'm working with immigration to have all the women inside deported. She's not happy with me either."

"Don't let that get to you, Maddie." Dwight rested a soothing hand on her shoulder. "You absolutely did the right thing." He lowered his voice and leaned forward. "You're not very popular with your boyfriend right now either, for the record. I might give him a wide berth if I were you."

Maddie flicked her eyes to Nick, her stomach clenching at the dark expression on his face. "I can see that."

"I'm just giving you a heads up." Dwight straightened "Can you take me inside?"

"Yes, but several of the women have already run. The one we're interested in is still there, and the good news is that her English is pretty good. I told her you were coming ... and that deporting her wouldn't be your first choice. I also told her I couldn't guarantee anything so I'm hoping that doesn't put you in an awkward position."

"We'll figure it out." Dwight climbed the first step, his frame stiffening when Sage appeared in the open doorway. "Speaking of wide berths and being popular," he muttered.

"Hi, Daddy." Sage flashed an innocent smile that would've caused Maddie to laugh under different circumstances. "I'm so happy to see you."

"Save it." Dwight held up his hand and glared at his daughter. "You're in big trouble, young lady. I mean ... the biggest. If they had a measuring stick for trouble, yours would be off the charts."

Sage, clearly a master at manipulating her father's emotions, jutted out her lower lip. "I was trying to help."

"And clearly you did," Dwight snapped. "You helped so much Maddie had to get involved and now you've gotten her in trouble."

Sage balked. "How did I get Maddie in trouble? She turned on me and insisted on calling you."

Maddie bit back a sigh. "I didn't turn on you. This is above our paygrade, though. We seriously needed help, and Dwight and Nick are the only two people I knew who could offer it."

"Oh, don't bring me into this," Nick drawled, sarcasm practically dripping from his tongue. "You didn't call me. You called Dwight. He's the one who will be offering you help today. I'm simply here to bear witness."

Maddie slid Nick a sidelong look. "I thought I should call him because this is his jurisdiction."

"Good answer." Nick kept his gaze averted. "Are we going inside or what?"

"Nicky ... ." Maddie reached out and tried not to cringe when he jerked his hand away from her.

"We should go inside," Nick pressed. "I'm sure we've got a long afternoon of questions ahead of us."

"Yes, thanks to Maddie," Sage sneered. "We can all thank her for this."

Maddie pressed the heel of her hand to her forehead. "Wow. And I thought I felt unpopular in high school."

"Don't you dare blame Maddie for this," Dwight warned. "You're in big trouble, Sage, and she did the absolute right thing."

"Except she was supposed to be at the hospital," Nick muttered. "The right thing would've been to call me when Sage approached her at the hospital."

"I felt trapped," Maddie whined. "She was so earnest and she said all this stuff about me helping the downtrodden. She trapped me."

"Oh, right, blame it on me," Sage seethed. "I'm the one who told you it was a secret and yet you couldn't wait to share it with my father. You're not much of a secret keeper."

"Knock that off," Dwight warned, extending a finger. "Maddie is the only reason I'm not grounding the crap out of you right now, although I haven't ruled it out for later."

"I'm an adult," Sage argued. "You can't ground an adult."

"Watch me."

Maddie risked a glance at Nick, hoping to see a smile curving his lips or a softening of the eyes. He didn't so much as glance at her, though, and his jawline looked as if it were carved out of granite as he stared straight forward.

"We need to talk to the woman inside," Nick reminded them.

"She could be escaping out the back as we're standing here and talking about this. We need to move."

"You're right." Dwight took the lead, Sage close on his heels. "We need to be gentle but firm. We need answers."

"Don't you dare arrest any of these women," Sage hissed. "I'll never forgive you if you do."

"You're not in the position to threaten me with anything," Dwight fired back. "You're in big trouble."

"I'm too old to be in trouble."

"I don't think your mother is going to feel that way."

Sage blanched. "You wouldn't dare tell my mother!"

"Watch me."

MADDIE LED DWIGHT AND Nick to the young woman in the corner. She hid under a pile of blankets, a bout of terrible shakes bombarding her body. Mercedes sat next to her, absolute murder coloring her features, but both women remained where they were sitting and didn't bother running despite the presence of two cops.

Dwight introduced himself, offering up an easy smile as he sat on the ground across from the girl. He wanted to appear as non-threatening as possible, and hunkering low was his best option. Since Nick was so tall, he followed suit, positioning himself right behind Dwight. Maddie considered sitting next to him, but the "no trespassing" sign Nick had clearly erected forced her to take a step away from him.

"This is Paloma," Mercedes said, her eyes grave. "She is terrified and wanted to run, but her health won't allow it. I'm certain this will end badly for both of us, but we will answer your questions in the hope that you won't punish us for being honest."

Dwight stared at her for a long beat. "I don't want to punish you at all," he said truthfully. "I understand that you're in a tough position here and I want to do what I can. That includes helping Paloma."

Paloma's shaking increased and Maddie momentarily discarded her worry regarding Nick and moved closer to the girl, searching through the ragged blankets until she came up with a pasty wrist and pressing her fingers to Paloma's pulse point.

Nick watched with mild interest, but he didn't offer up a smile to ease Maddie's worry.

"I need you to tell me a little about yourself, Paloma," Dwight prodded. "When did you get here?"

The girl looked so timid, the trembles causing her whole body to shake so violently that Maddie had to fight the urge to wrap her arms around the girl and offer solace.

"I've been here for several years," Paloma said after a beat. "It feels longer sometimes."

"I imagine." Dwight was calm and amiable. He kept his motions short and shallow so as not to alarm her. "You came from Mexico?"

"My parents died when I was thirteen," Paloma explained. "I tried to keep my brothers and sisters together, but it didn't happen. I couldn't go into any of the homes because I was too old, and after several months living on the street the police made sure I understood that I would have to go.

"I didn't have a lot of options and because of my age I could not get a job," she continued. "One day a man approached me on the street. He said he could make me a model. I'm not stupid enough to say I believed him, but I took a chance because I thought if I could get settled in America then eventually I would be able to bring my brothers and sisters here."

"I take it that's not what happened," Dwight prodded.

Paloma shook her head. "The border crossing was in the middle of the night. They made us walk for miles and if you fell behind you were left. I lost track of where I was, basically put one foot in front of the other, and I kept going. I made it.

"My first job was in Arizona," she continued. "I cleaned house for a woman with cold eyes. It was a lot of work – I never saw a house that huge before – but I thought it would be okay. I thought I would survive. Then her husband came home from prison to live at the house and I realized they expected something else from me."

Maddie's stomach twisted as she fought off tears. Nick saw the struggle and almost reached out to her. He was so angry, though, he thought better of it. They had a long talk ahead of them and he didn't want to taint it before he had a chance to express what he considered totally justifiable fury.

"The house turned into hell after that," Paloma said. "I learned better English, which was the only thing that made things tolerable, and then the wife decided the husband was too attached to me and sent me away. I thought things would get better. I was foolish."

"When did you arrive in Detroit?" Dwight queried.

"Two years ago. I was in Chicago before then."

"Doing what?"

"I would rather not talk about it."

Dwight opened his mouth to argue, but Maddie offered up a firm headshake to quiet him.

"You don't have to talk about it." Maddie moved her hand to the girl's forehead. "You have a fever."

"I'm fine."

"I don't think you are," Maddie pressed. "You're shaking really badly and there's a hitch to your breathing. Your pulse is thready and elevated. I think you should go to the hospital."

The look Paloma shot Maddie was one of pure venom. "And what makes you think I would ever go to the hospital? The monster lives there."

Maddie had the grace to be abashed. "I'm sorry. I forgot about that."

"You forgot?" Paloma was incredulous. "It must be nice to have the option to forget. Me, I will never forget."

"I need to hear your story," Dwight said gently. "I need to know exactly what happened and why you think the individual who attacked you is the same person who dropped the bodies in the lot."

"It was six months ago or so," Paloma said, dragging her ferocious glare from Maddie and focusing on Dwight. "Maybe it was only five months. I lose track of time. It was after we started hearing about girls like us going missing."

"What did you hear?" Nick was genuinely curious. "You guys

usually get the story first, so I'm curious what you heard before it took on a life of its own."

"It was just whispers really," Paloma replied. "We heard first that a girl – her name was Betsy – was taken right from the corner. She was screaming and fighting, clawing and biting, and yet no one came to help."

"You have to understand that we hear stories like this all the time," Mercedes interjected. "The pimps and runners spread them to make us afraid to run. They want us to believe they're our only way to survive."

"I understand. What happened next?"

"I didn't think much of it," Paloma answered. "I had been working as an independent for three months. I was terrified my former pimp would find me, but so far he'd stayed away. That didn't mean I was relaxed, though. I was coming home from a particularly ... um, what is the word I'm looking for?" She turned to Mercedes for help.

"Vigorous," Mercedes supplied. "Your client that night was vigorous. He left bruises on you and a couple of cuts on your arms and legs."

Maddie barely managed to muffle a sob as a tear slid down her cheek. Her reaction was almost enough to undo Nick, but he managed to hold it together.

"I was bleeding and I knew they wouldn't let me on the People Mover if I was bleeding so I was trying to clean up when a man came around the corner and saw me," Paloma said. "It was dark so I didn't get a good look at him before you ask. There were no lights. It was on the street where they always turn off the light."

"They turn the lights off?" Nick asked, confused.

"It's a way to save money," Dwight explained. "It's absolutely ridiculous, but they turn off the lights in some areas. Of course, those are the areas that most need lights."

"It was very dark and there were no cars but I wasn't afraid," Paloma said. "The man was nice and he was ... um ... sweet. Wait. I don't think that's the word. He made noises that he was sad for me and wanted to help."

"He was sympathetic," Maddie offered helpfully.

Paloma bobbed her head. "He was sympathetic and he had some stuff in the bag he carried," she said. "He cleaned up the wounds and talked to me like I was a real person rather than what I really was. He was nice and offered to buy me dinner. I thought he was a good person so I agreed."

"Then what happened?" Dwight asked.

"I thought we would walk, but he pointed me toward his car. I knew there was something wrong with the car right away, though, because it had no inside handle on the door. I noticed that right away. That's one of the things we're warned about."

"No handle?" Nick rubbed his forehead. "That was something that Bundy pulled back when he was killing girls."

"Yeah, and it's not something most women would overlook," Dwight said. "Because he's a doctor, he probably figures he can get away with it."

"Did he tell you he was a doctor?" Maddie asked. "I mean ... did he say those words?"

"Yes. That's why he had the bag and wanted to help."

"What happened when you saw the car had no door handle on the inside?" Dwight asked. "Did you make a fuss or get in?"

"I knew better than getting in," Paloma supplied. "The second I saw there was no handle I knew I was in trouble. I tried to look at his face, but the lights were dim in the car and I only saw a shadow over his jawline. There was something there, though, something scary. I knew I would be in trouble if I didn't think fast.

"I acted as if I was going to get in the car, but then I purposely dropped my small bag before getting in," she continued. "He made a big show of getting it for me and I pretended to almost fall so I could take a step back. The second he bent over I ran."

"Did he try to stop you?"

"Yes."

"You obviously got away, though," Dwight pointed out.

"I knew the streets better than him and managed to hide in a building," Paloma said. "I watched him for a full hour. He waited for me to return. I could see the way he moved, the way he hunted. He was angry he lost me and he kept kicking his car. Finally he gave up and went away.

"Even after that I waited another hour to be sure," she continued. "I was too frightened to leave."

"That's a terrible story," Dwight said. "I think you were lucky to get away."

"Even though I lost my purse."

"Even though," Dwight agreed. "I have to ask you, how do you know the person who tried to grab you is the same one who was dumping bodies in the lot?"

"Because two weeks ago I was walking by that parcel late at night," Paloma explained. "It was later than I like to be out – almost three – but I wasn't too worried because the lights were on. I always feel safer when the lights are on."

"Okay."

"I was walking by the lot when I heard a noise. I looked to the left, but all I could see was a dark shape. It was too far away, but I could see a bunch of those wood things ... what do you call them?"

"Pallets," Mercedes supplied.

"Yes, pallets," Paloma said. "I could see them and people said after that the bodies were found underneath them. Anyway, I was walking past when the man called out to me. He knew my name and I recognized his voice. It was the man from the car.

"He frightened me so I did the only thing I could do," she continued. "I started to run and I did not look back. I never looked back."

"And you're absolutely certain it was him?" Dwight pressed.

Paloma nodded. "You never forget the devil's voice once you hear it. I am certain."

"That's good enough for me." Dwight raised his eyes until they snagged with Maddie's. "We need to get photos so Paloma can look at them."

"Before that we need to get her medical help," Maddie said. "I'm pretty sure she's fighting off pneumonia. If she won't go to the hospital, we have to find another way to treat her."

"I will not go to the hospital." Paloma was firm. "The monster is there."

"Then I'm going to have to think of something else," Maddie muttered, even though she had no idea what that solution would possibly be. "She needs help and we're the only ones who can give it to her."

15. FIFTEEN

Ultimately Maddie came up with a plan that she considered a tolerable compromise. Since the only person who still appeared to like her was Dwight, he congratulated her on the idea and helped her convince several nurses from the hospital to come to them rather than trying to force the terrified women to go to a hospital where a killer might be roaming.

Andrea, Iris, and Sandy made the trek, eyebrows arched, and when they saw what was happening inside the abandoned building they immediately set to work.

"I didn't even know this was happening here," Andrea said, making a clucking sound as she shook her head. "This makes me all kinds of sad."

"You and me both," Maddie said. "I want to see if we can get around to everyone who stayed, but I'm pretty sure Paloma over there has pneumonia to start with."

Andrea tilted her head to the side as she surveyed the pale woman in question. "Maddie, if she has pneumonia, we need to get her to the hospital."

"I know that. She won't go."

Andrea moved her mouth a few times but no sound came out.

Maddie could tell the woman was gearing up to argue so she cut her off.

"She's afraid of the hospital," Maddie explained. "She thinks a doctor there tried to attack her a few months ago."

Andrea's eyes widened. "Seriously?"

Maddie nodded. "It's a long story and I'm not sure how everything is going to come together, but I believe her."

"Okay, what doctor?" Andrea asked, turning pragmatic. "I can check the schedule and arrange to get her in when he's not there."

"That's just the thing. We don't know. She didn't get a good look at his face, although she did hear his voice and I think she'll be able to identify him that way. She won't go to the hospital, though. She's terrified."

"She might feel differently if she dies here. This place isn't conducive to recovery from pneumonia. We brought basic supplies because we weren't sure what you needed."

"I'm really appreciative of that. I know it's a big hassle."

Andrea waved off the words. "We're fine helping. We know you wouldn't ask unless it was a big deal. It's just ... it's sad. It's weird and it's sad."

"Yeah, you have no idea how weird it really is."

"Why don't you tell me as we're working our way through these girls. I have a feeling that more than one of them needs help."

"That sounds like a plan."

NICK STOOD AGAINST THE far wall, arms crossed over his muscled chest, and watched Maddie work with her former friends. His blond seemed intense and diligent, but he didn't miss the occasional worried glances she tossed in his direction.

Nick wasn't the vengeful sort so part of him wanted to reassure Maddie that everything would be okay. The other part, the angry part, wanted to grab her by the shoulders and shake. He was furious and he couldn't seem to get past the emotion. For now, he believed the best thing he could do for Maddie was keep his distance until he cooled down.

Dwight apparently had other intentions.

"How long are you going to pout?"

Nick scowled as he slid his gaze to the Detroit police detective. "I'm not pouting."

"That's exactly what you're doing," Dwight countered. "You're punishing her."

Nick balked. "I most certainly am not punishing her."

"You are. You might not want to admit it, but you are."

"Well, if I am, she has it coming," Nick grumbled, glaring at his shoes. "She lied to me."

"She didn't lie to you," Dwight scoffed. "She was on her way to the hospital when Sage ambushed her. This is on Sage. Maddie didn't do anything wrong. In fact, when she realized what was going on, she did everything right."

"She should've called me the second Sage approached her," Nick argued. "We agreed that she would be at the hospital during the morning hours and then find me at the police station. That was our compromise."

Dwight gave Nick a long look. "What are you angry about? I mean ... really. What is it that has your panties in a twist?"

"If you're trying to direct my anger at you so I'll forgive Maddie, good job. I kind of want to punch you right now."

"I would gladly take it if I thought it meant you would stop punishing her."

"I'm not punishing her!"

"You are," Dwight challenged. "You think I don't get it, but I do. Why do you think I'm so angry with Sage?"

"Because she lied and put herself in danger."

"It's not anger fueling me, though," Dwight said. "Not really. What's fueling me is fear because I know what could've happened to Sage if she ran into the wrong person down here. I'm still not sure how she found these women – and you can believe I'm going to find out – but I'm more afraid for my daughter than angry at her. I think that's your problem."

Nick tilted his head to the side, considering. "No. She lied to me."

"Fine. Be stubborn." Dwight pushed himself away from the wall. "I just want you to remember something you told me a few months ago. I don't remember the exact phrasing, but you basically said that the most important thing in the world to you was loving Maddie. I remember thinking it was odd for you to say it the way you did. I mean, I understood what you meant, but at the time you were worried about her safety, too.

"I know you love her and I haven't doubted that since the moment you called me asking questions," he continued. "I sensed something in the way you fretted over the phone. I don't know what, but it was definitely there. I think it's normal to worry about the person you love, but is worrying about Maddie to the point where you're trying to punish her what's best for her?"

Nick let loose with a derisive snort. "I know you don't believe it, but I'm honestly not punishing her. I'm keeping my distance because I'm upset and angry. I don't want to take it out on her. That's why I'm over here."

Dwight didn't look convinced. "You're not punishing her at all?"

"No. I don't want to yell and frighten her. She doesn't deserve that."

"You're going to yell at her a bit later, though, aren't you?"

"We're going to have a serious discussion about why she didn't call me," Nick corrected. "I have no intention of yelling at her."

Nick's aggressive stance told Dwight otherwise.

"Just remember that you love her more than anything," Dwight supplied. "Remember how miserable you were without her. Remember how miserable she was without you. You two are spending a lifetime together and there are always going to be fights. Make sure you keep the love at the forefront when you have those fights. It will lead to fewer regrets."

"Are you giving me that advice from experience?"

"I am a perfect husband and have never upset my wife. I have no idea what you're talking about."

Nick couldn't swallow his chuckle. "Yeah. I'll take your advice to heart."

"Do that. Maddie was caught in a bad situation because of Sage. Maddie didn't create the situation and she did the right thing. She shouldn't be penalized for that."

Nick heaved out a sigh. "I'm not going to penalize her. I am going to talk to her. I think it's necessary."

"Son, when you get to be my age, you're going to realize all these fights you thought were necessary when you were in your twenties are complete and total crap," Dwight said. "Still, everyone needs to go through it. Don't let your anger get the better of you, though. If you let this fight fester, it will affect both of you."

"It's going to be okay." Nick found it odd that he was trying to make Dwight feel better given the circumstances, but he didn't dwell on it. "Maddie and I will be fine. We always survive fights. This will be no different."

"Uh-huh." Dwight's expression was dubious. "And exactly how many fights have you guys had? I'm going to be honest, I don't think it's many. You two are far too in love with each other and kissing constantly to fight."

"We've fought."

"How often?"

"At least once or twice."

Dwight snorted. "That's what I thought. Make this one a short one. Once Maddie and her friends work through these women, we have some decisions to make."

Nick nodded. "I know. What do you make of Paloma's story?"

Dwight was happy to change the subject. "I believe her."

"I do, too. That means one of the doctors at the hospital is very likely a killer. You realize that, right?"

"You're thinking that one of the members of Maddie's fan club might be the culprit."

"I don't know that I believe that," Nick cautioned. "It's easy for me to lean that way, but I don't want to because it might mean overlooking the obvious."

"I get what you're saying and it would seem somehow easier for us if Tipton or Bishop was to blame, but we have to take this one step at a time," Dwight said. "We need to get photos in front of Paloma."

"You heard her. She didn't see his face well. We need her to listen to voices."

Dwight was uncomfortable with the suggestion. "I don't think she's going to agree to that and I feel bad asking it of her."

"Then maybe we should have Maddie ask," Nick suggested. "She's already everyone's least favorite person, at least in this building. Maybe she won't mind being the bad guy again."

"You're not going to gloat about that, are you?"

Nick shrugged. "She's still my favorite person, even if I am irritated."

"Then perhaps we should have a talk with her," Dwight said. "We're starting to get into a weird spot here. We have someone who might be able to point us in the right direction, but she's unwilling to take the chance. We have to figure out a way to change her mind."

"I'm open to suggestions."

"OKAY, YOU'RE REALLY SICK."

Andrea was never one to mince words so she gave it to Paloma straight.

For her part, the young woman merely blinked as she regarded the worried nurse. "Isn't that why you're here?"

"Yes, but I'm not a doctor."

"I don't like doctors."

Andrea looked to Maddie for help. "Maddie, she needs intravenous fluids. She needs boosters. I can't give her any of that here."

Maddie rubbed her thumb over her lower lip. "I know." She didn't bother faking enthusiasm when she turned and knelt next to Paloma. "You have to go to the hospital. I know you don't want to, but it's necessary."

Paloma immediately started shaking her head. "I won't."

"You have to."

"I won't!" Paloma screeched out the words, drawing Nick's attention as he crossed the room.

Nick changed course, making up his mind on the spot, and approached the three women. "What's going on?"

"She's sick," Andrea replied without hesitation. "I mean ... really sick. Her lungs are compromised. Her immune system is almost nonexistent. She's exhausted, malnourished, and worn down. We need to get her admitted to the hospital and on a treatment program right away."

"I won't go." Paloma was firm. "He's there. The devil is there."

Nick briefly locked gazes with Maddie, something unsaid passing between them, and then dropped to a crouch so he could be at eye level with Paloma. "I understand you're frightened."

"I'm more than frightened," Paloma shot back. "I will die if I go there. I know it. He's there and he's waiting for me."

"I think you're giving him more power than he's earned, but we can work through this together." Nick dug deep to remain calm, calling on his training to work through the fraught situation. "I will be with you the whole time. We'll make sure you're never alone and get a few officers to sit by your bed to be sure.

"The truth is, it's better for us if you're in the hospital because you'll be able to identify the voice we're looking for," he continued. "You're very important to us. I swear it. We won't abandon you."

Paloma licked her lips as she turned to Mercedes. "I don't know. What do you think?"

"I think they're obviously worried," Mercedes said without hesitation. "That means you need help. If they're willing to give it, I don't see where we're in a position to say no."

Paloma heaved out a sigh and leaned back her head. "Fine. If I die, though, I will haunt you to the end of time."

Since Maddie could see and talk to ghosts, she had no trouble believing that. "We won't let you die."

. . .

MERCEDES RODE IN THE ambulance with Paloma, which left Maddie and Nick to hurry to the hospital. Dwight stayed behind with Iris and Sandy to work through the rest of the women and promised to head toward the hospital as soon as possible.

Maddie and Nick picked a brisk pace for their walk. Nick was hopeful that meant they wouldn't talk, but Maddie refused to let the moment escape.

"I'm sorry. I know you're angry and I don't blame you, but it all happened so fast. I didn't mean to upset you."

"Oh, geez." Nick pinched the bridge of his nose as he walked. "I don't think now is the time for this conversation."

"Oh." Maddie's eyes filled with despair. "Does that mean you're going to keep pretending I'm not someone worthy of talking to?"

Nick heaved out a sigh. "That's not what I've been doing."

"It is. You won't even look at me."

"That's because I'm angry and I don't want to yell at you," Nick supplied. "I would think you'd understand that."

"I do understand that, but I would rather you yell and get it out of your system." Maddie didn't want to admit it, but the fact Nick refused to touch her was turning into a dull ache. He was generally tactile and couldn't get enough of her and even though she knew it made her pathetic and whiny, Maddie yearned for some form of contact. "I can't stand it that you won't touch me."

Nick slowed his pace and pinned her with a gaze. "What?"

"You won't touch me. You usually do something ... even if it's just a hand to my back or a squeeze of my fingers. Right now you simply won't touch me ... and I don't like it."

"That's because I'm angry, Maddie."

"I know but ... ."

"No." Nick wagged a finger and shook his head. "We're going to talk about the decision you made and why it was a mistake, and we're going to do it at a time when I don't feel pressure to give you what you want simply because you're clearly miserable.

"I get it, Mad, you didn't mean for this to happen," he continued. "Still, you knew I was worried about you running all over the place given everything that was going on. We compromised even though I wasn't comfortable with it. You should've called me when Sage showed up."

"I know. I wanted to. It's just ... she was so serious."

"Well, I'm serious, too," Nick said. "I'm upset, Mad. I'm not simply going to let you get away with breaking your word to me."

"That's not what I was doing," Maddie protested. "I was trying to help Sage. Then, when she showed me what I was dealing with, I wanted to help those women. If you expect me to apologize for that, I won't. They needed help."

"I don't expect you to apologize for *that*," Nick clarified. "I do, however, feel I'm owed an apology."

"You are," Maddie agreed. "I should've figured out a different way to keep you in the loop and help Sage at the same time. I wish I had and I'm so sorry you feel as if I did this to purposely hurt you. I would never do that."

Nick felt his resolve ebbing in the face of her sadness. "I know you wouldn't purposely hurt me."

"I got caught up," Maddie added. "Sage needed help and she laid all of this 'I thought you wanted to help those in need' stuff on me. I melted even though I probably shouldn't have done it. I can't help it. Sometimes I'm a marshmallow."

Even though he was determined to be stern, Nick let loose with a hearty chuckle. "You're my marshmallow, you big manipulator." He grabbed her by the arm and tugged her to him, wrapping his arms around and her and grinning when he heard her make a purring sound as she burrowed her face in the hollow of his neck. "I love you, Maddie. That's never going to change. Even when we fight, I'm always going to love you."

"Even if you don't want to touch me?"

"Mad, I always want to touch you. The reason I stayed away is because I was angry and I knew I would be the one turning into a marshmallow the second you batted those eyes at me."

"I love you, Nicky. I'm sorry. I'll do better."

"I just want you safe, Maddie." He tilted up her chin and kissed her upturned mouth. "Just think next time before you wander away in a big city. What would've happened if you ran into trouble, love? I wouldn't have known where to start looking for you."

"I ... don't know. I'm really sorry, though."

"I know you are. I forgive you." He pulled her in for a second hug. "I'm definitely the marshmallow. We both recognize that, right?"

"I like you when you're a marshmallow."

"Yeah, yeah, yeah."

16. SIXTEEN

Paloma was a nervous wreck at the hospital. Nick positioned himself so he was constantly by her side, a soothing and calm face for her to focus on. When the emergency team tried to remove him from her room, Paloma became so distressed they stopped trying.

Maddie was glad for his steadying presence even though Paloma gripped his hand so hard she worried the terrified woman might rip it from his arm.

"She seems like she would do better under sedation," Andrea noted, moving to Maddie's side.

"I know, but she's not going to allow that and I refuse to force it on her." Maddie rolled her neck as she watched a female doctor – Nick made a direct request for that – inject Paloma with an initial booster. "She's been through enough. She doesn't need to have her choice taken from her."

"Yeah, well, I'm going to need some information for the intake forms," Andrea supplied. "I know something odd is going on here, but I'm going to need some sort of explanation that will fly should the hospital brass question me."

Maddie expected that and nodded. "Wait one second and we'll go to the lobby and talk. I just need to tell Nick where I'll be."

"Okay."

Maddie gave the attendants a wide berth as she circled the bed, not stopping until she was at Nick's side. "I need to help Andrea with information for some forms." She kept her voice low. "I'm going out in the lobby with her, but I won't be far."

Nick looked torn. "Do you think that's a good idea? What if word spreads why she's here?"

"I don't see where we have another option. The hospital has rules and they need information. I'll do my best to vague it up, but Paloma is going to need to be here for at least forty-eight hours."

"I know. I called Dwight and he's working on getting uniformed officers here to keep her safe. He hopes to join us within the hour. He said two at the most."

Maddie didn't want to ask the obvious question, but she didn't have a choice. "Is he turning them over to immigration?"

"I don't know, Mad." Nick offered up a helpless shrug. "He's going to do the very best that he can. Show him a little faith. You never know how things might work out."

Maddie gave his free hand a squeeze. "Sometimes they work out better than you can possibly hope."

Nick grinned. "They really do."

"I promise not to leave the lobby for anything other than a bathroom break," Maddie offered. "I won't screw up twice in one day."

Nick eyed her for a long beat. "Make sure you don't." He gave her a quick kiss. "Don't wander too far. I'll know if you do."

"Yeah, yeah."

ANDREA WAITED FOR Maddie in the lobby, a folder full of forms sitting in front of her. Despite the serious nature of the situation, she appeared to be in a good mood.

"So, you're still the conquering hero for the downtrodden, huh?"

Maddie held her hands up and shrugged. "I do the best I can." She took the seat opposite Andrea and let loose with a long sigh. "It's not even noon yet and I feel wiped. I don't miss days like this."

"And what do you do with your days now?" Andrea asked. "I'm guessing that tall hunk of man you have following you around makes up for some of your time."

Maddie smirked. "Just a little."

"Did you meet him when you moved back north?"

"Oh, no. I've known Nick since kindergarten. He's the best friend I've ever had."

Andrea was clearly surprised by the admission. "How come he never visited you down here?"

The answer to that question was long and convoluted so Maddie decided to truncate it. "We had a falling out after high school. We didn't talk for a bit. As soon as I hit Blackstone Bay, though, we started talking again."

"It looks as if things have worked out for you."

"They definitely have."

Andrea tapped her finger against Maddie's engagement ring. "You guys clearly work fast. When did he propose?"

"Christmas."

"Oh, how romantic." Andrea made a funny face as she batted her eyelashes. "You guys are just too cute for school."

"Ha, ha." Maddie rolled her neck as she tried to get comfortable in the hard plastic chair. "So, what do you need from me on the forms?"

"Well, I'm guessing we're going to need to be creative," Andrea said, sobering. "I realize that our new friend is illegal – and so were the bulk of the women at the library – but we have funds to cover stuff like that. We need to come up with an appropriate story for how we got there, though."

"I called you. Can't you blame it on me?"

"I would feel better if we could say that we got an anonymous call."

"That would be a lie, though." Maddie wasn't comfortable with that suggestion. "Tell the truth. If there's an issue, well, I'll find a way to cover the bill. It might take me some time, but I don't want to lie."

"Let's hope it doesn't come to that." Andrea tapped the tip of the pen against the paperwork. "Off the record, though, can you tell me what happened?"

Maddie nodded without hesitation. "It's a long and convoluted story. How much time do you have?"

"Enough to hear it all."

"Okay, brace yourself. Things are about to get ugly."

SAGE FOUND NICK IN Paloma's room when she hit the hospital. After a long and nasty fight with her father – one that ended with him issuing a bevy of threats she couldn't help but wonder if he intended to make good on – she insisted on following up on Paloma's care. Dwight wasn't happy with her adamant demands, but he didn't put up too much of a fight. He figured she should be able to see this through to the end, whatever the end may be.

"How is she doing?" Sage asked, keeping her voice low because she realized Paloma was slumbering. "Did they knock her out?"

Nick shook his head as he loosely held Paloma's hand. "She's exhausted. They've been pumping fluids and booster shots into her. The doctor said that they were going to have to start medicating her soon, but she was trying to figure out the best way to do it without overloading Paloma's system. She's extremely weak."

"She's been sick for more than a week," Sage noted. "I should've tried to get her to the doctor sooner."

"You definitely should have," Dwight agreed, glowering. "In fact, the second you happened upon them you should have come to me for help."

"Oh, geez." Sage rolled her eyes as only a put-upon daughter could do. "Are we going to argue about this again? You've made it very clear that I was an idiot and you're disappointed in me."

Dwight met his daughter's gaze with an even one of his own. "I didn't say I was disappointed in you."

"I believe that's what we argued about for the entire trip to the hospital."

"No, I said I was disappointed that you didn't feel that you could trust me with your secret," Dwight corrected. "I didn't say I was disappointed that you have a big heart and wanted to help."

Sage was taken aback. "I ... well ... um ... ."

"Yeah, I'm not such an ogre now, am I?" Dwight made a tsking sound and shuffled his feet. "You're a good girl, Sage. You always have been. I'm not upset that you wanted to help. I wish you would've realized those women needed more help than you could give, but I'm not disappointed in you."

"Oh, well ... ." Sage was sheepish. "I'm sorry that I didn't come to you right away, if it's any consolation. Knowing how sick Paloma is and that she could've died from this ... well ... I feel like a bit of a ninny."

"That's normal for you." Dwight flicked her ear. "I still want to know how you stumbled across them."

"It's not much of a story," Sage said. "I was at the Wayne State campus library because I needed to check out a book and they didn't have an electronic version. I saw Mercedes struggling with two big bags of food when I left and offered to help. She didn't look as if she wanted to trust me, but she didn't have a lot of choice so she showed me to the other library – the closed one – and it just sort of spiraled from there."

"When did you realize that my case might overlap with the women you found?"

"Not until yesterday when I heard you talking about it," Sage replied. "You didn't go into a lot of details, but I heard Paloma's story about three days ago. I thought it sounded similar so I thought maybe Maddie could help because she's ... well ... different. Instead of helping, though, she totally turned on us."

"Hey, don't say that." Nick gave the girl a fierce look. "Maddie did the right thing."

"Then why are you angry at her?"

"Because she should've called and told me she was leaving the hospital. As soon as she realized how serious things were, she called Dwight. I'm still mildly irritated that she called him instead of me, but she got the job done and didn't wait around for things to spiral so far they were out of our control."

Sage worked her jaw, frustration evident. "You're just taking her side because you're engaged. You're mad at her. I know it."

"I was irritated with her," Nick clarified. "As for taking her side, I know she did the best she could. We've talked it out and we're fine."

"Have you now?" Dwight looked smug. "I wonder what gave you the idea to do that."

"It wasn't you. I just can't stay mad at her. She says she's a big marshmallow and that's why she went with Sage, no questions asked, but I think I'm the marshmallow."

"You're both marshmallows," Dwight said. "The thing we have to do now is run the doctors in this place. It's not going to be easy, but it has to be done. Once we have some photos, we can start showing them to Paloma."

"She said she didn't get a good look at his face, though," Sage reminded him. "She might not be able to identify him."

"We have to start somewhere and I think this is the best spot. I don't know what else to do."

"So let's do it," Nick said. "It's something we can do in here while keeping watch. No matter what, I think the one thing we can agree on is that Paloma can't be left alone."

"We definitely agree there," Dwight agreed. "I have an advocate from immigration heading this way in a few hours. We'll tackle one problem at a time."

"And what about the others?" Nick asked. "Do you have an advocate for them?"

"Oh, well, it's the funniest thing." Dwight rubbed his chin and adopted an innocent expression. "It seems that while I was talking on the phone to my unit, the women staying in that building snuck out and I didn't even see it happen. Apparently they took their medication and ran. I'm stumped about what to do about it."

Nick barely managed to contain his smirk. "Huh. Imagine that."

"I know. I'm going to get grief about it at the precinct, but there were simply too many women to watch and I got distracted."

"I wouldn't worry about being the big marshmallow, Nick," Sage said dryly. "I think Dad has that titled locked up."

"You're still grounded," Dwight warned. "I wouldn't push things too far."

Sage didn't look remotely frightened. "I'll keep that in mind."

"THAT'S QUITE THE STORY," Andrea said, her face ashen when Maddie wrapped up her tale. "I don't even know what to make of it."

"It's terrible," Maddie agreed. "We don't know what to do. Paloma is convinced it's one of the doctors here who attacked her."

"Do you believe her?"

"What reason does she have to lie?"

"I can think of several reasons," Andrea supplied. "The first would be that she's illegal and wants to gain some sympathy from the higher-ups when it comes to pleading her case for asylum. Have you considered that?"

"Not really. I can't imagine what good that would've done her when she told a young woman that story days ago. To my knowledge, she had no idea Sage was affiliated with a police detective. What benefit could Sage be to her?"

"I guess that's fair." Andrea's expression was thoughtful. "I honestly don't know what to make of this story. I lean toward dismissing it, though. I can tell you're going the other way."

"I am," Maddie confirmed. "I believe something very bad is happening on the streets. I also think that Paloma had something terrible happen to her, and in the neighborhood in question. I can't disregard those two things even though you don't think they're connected."

"I didn't say that I didn't believe they were connected," Andrea clarified. "I just have trouble believing the entire thing. Perhaps that's because it's hard for me to imagine that someone I work with could be a murderer."

"I understand the feeling. Believe me, I get it. I've been surprised at the evil residing inside seemingly normal people for a while now.

That doesn't mean it's not happening. I don't think we can afford to turn our backs on a potential serial killer."

"Serial killer?" Andrea's eyebrows flew up her forehead. "You can't be serious."

"We have twenty dead women and more missing. What would you call it?"

"I don't know, but a serial killer is ... well ... it's guys like Dahmer and Bundy. It's adults who dress up like clowns and creep people out. It's not a doctor who's responsible for saving lives. If we really had a serial killer here, don't you think we would know it? Wouldn't we have a rash of dead bodies to contend with ourselves?"

"That's a good point, but I don't think all serial killers work the same way," Maddie explained. "Some serial killers are angels of death, like you would see at a hospital. Others, though, they're brutal hunters. That seems to be what we're dealing with here.

"If we have a hunter, which I definitely believe we do, killing someone when they're unconscious on an operating table or knocked out in a bed wouldn't hold the same thrill," she continued. "I think the person we're dealing with needs to hunt. It's probably primordial for him."

"Okay, let's say I believe you," Andrea hedged. "How do you plan on hunting this person down. You said that Paloma can't identify him by sight. How is she going to be able to help?"

"She would recognize his voice, which would give us a start."

"But what if she doesn't hear him?"

"Then I don't know." Maddie felt mildly helpless. "I just know we have to narrow down our options. To do that, we need to come up with a suspect pool and work from there."

"And how do you plan on doing that?"

"Well, for starters, I thought you might be able to help me."

Andrea balked at Maddie's impish grin. "I can already tell I'm going to hate this."

"Probably," Maddie agreed. "I won't badger you to help. If you say no, I'll respect your answer."

"I have to know your plan before I answer either way."

"I thought maybe you could get me into the file room," Maddie said. "I need to look at a few things and I obviously can't do it out in the open."

"No, I agree. The thing is, all of our files are electronic. You need a login code to do it, and as fond as I am of you, I don't feel comfortable handing over my login information."

"And I totally get that. It's almost lunchtime, though."

Andrea furrowed her brow. "So?"

"So I thought we could get some soup, head into the records room, and I might accidentally see something while looking over your shoulder," she suggested. "That way we wouldn't technically be breaking any rules."

"We would be breaking the rule about civilians being in the file room."

"Okay, one little rule."

Andrea heaved out a sigh as she rubbed her forehead, her mind clearly busy. "I don't know."

"I don't want to put you on the spot." Maddie meant it. "If you're not comfortable then I'll back away. I'll find a different way to track down information. I merely thought this would save us time."

"If we get caught, I could lose my job," Andrea pointed out.

"I know. It's not fair to ask. If we don't figure out who is doing this, though, a lot of other women could lose their lives. We're talking young women who could simply disappear from the street without anyone knowing."

"Oh, man." Andrea leaned back so she could stare at the ceiling. "You know exactly how to manipulate me, don't you?"

"I had it happen to me earlier. I understand that you don't like it. If you're uncomfortable, say no. That will be the end of it."

"Oh, right." Andrea's voice was almost a growl. "If I do nothing and another body dump site is located, I won't be able to live with myself. We both know it."

Actually, Maddie was banking on it. "It's not your responsibility. If you want to help, though, I'll gladly take it."

"Fine." Andrea threw up her hands in defeat. "I don't see what other option I have."

Maddie beamed. "You won't regret this."

"Yeah, somehow I don't think that's true. Let's do it, though. If I am working with a killer, I definitely want to know who it is."

17. SEVENTEEN

Maddie tipped off Nick to her plans before scurrying off with Andrea. He wasn't exactly thrilled that she was about to break the law, but he soothed himself with the knowledge that he was technically on vacation and outside of his jurisdiction, which meant he wasn't neglecting his duties. He had no doubt that upon further examination he would probably be angry with himself, though, but for now he let it go.

"Anything?" Dwight asked as he ran physician names on his laptop.

"Not really," Nick replied. He was forced to use his phone for the searches, which massively slowed him down. "I can't run deep searches on this thing."

"I could try to get you another laptop, but we'd have to go back to the precinct for that. I don't think it's a good idea until I've got bodies on the door to watch Paloma."

"I would rather stay close to the hospital," Nick admitted. "I don't want to be separated from Maddie again."

"I thought that was part of your normal thought process," Dwight teased. "Maddie is here so you have to be here, too. Separation is bad." He made a taunting face, but Nick wasn't bothered by the insinuation in the least.

"If you had a chance to hang out with an angel, would you pass it up?"

"Oh, gag me." Dwight found he enjoyed messing with Nick. The man was easygoing. He wasn't sure that would be the case the first time they shared a discussion – one in which Dwight was naturally suspicious about why Nick was trying to dig up information about Maddie – but he'd grown rather fond of the boy and couldn't imagine a better match for Maddie. Since he'd come to think of the woman as something of a surrogate daughter, it made him feel better to know that Nick would always be at her side.

That didn't mean he didn't enjoy teasing Nick.

"You're kind of a whipped puppy where Maddie is concerned, aren't you?"

Nick nodded without hesitation. "I am and I'm proud of it."

"You're a weird man."

"I can live with that." Nick scratched at the back of his neck as he stretched out his legs. "Maybe we're looking at this the wrong way. Have you considered that?"

"I always consider that. What do you mean, though?"

"I mean that they're doctors. The odds of them having criminal records are slim. If they did, it would've been found before they were hired. Whoever did this has managed to fly under the radar, and probably for a very long time."

"Okay, I get what you're saying." Dwight bobbed his head. "We still have to start looking somewhere. Where do you suggest looking?"

"The doctors themselves," Nick replied. "We need to dig into their personal lives."

"Can you give me an example?"

"Sure. Who works the late shift on a regular basis? I'm guessing that's not a popular shift. Our guy probably prefers it, though, because it allows him to hunt and dispose of bodies when the rest of the world is asleep."

"Huh." Dwight was impressed with his younger cohort's reasoning skills. "That makes a lot of sense. We need the hospital's schedule. I'm not sure that's something they're going to willingly hand over, though."

"Probably not. It's a good thing we have someone on the inside to do that for us, huh?"

"You mean Maddie."

"If she's going to break the law, she might as well go all out."

"See, I'm pretending you didn't say that. I don't want to know that she's breaking the law. To me she's a sweet and innocent girl who went off for some coffee."

"She's not all that innocent. She only looks it."

"Ugh. You've corrupted her. You and your filthy mind are ruining my illusions."

Nick chuckled. "You sound like her father."

"Yeah, you haven't mentioned much about him," Dwight noted. "I know that we haven't had a lot of time, but how did that come about?"

Nick told him the story, truncating it but not leaving anything out. When he was finished, Dwight was thoughtful.

"And you're okay with him?"

Nick shrugged. "I don't know that 'okay' is the word I would use," he hedged. "I think that Olivia was bitter about the split and did her best to keep George from Maddie. Now, don't get me wrong, I loved Olivia a great deal, but I don't think she did right by Maddie on that front. Maddie deserved to know her father."

"And you're sure the story he told you was true?"

Nick nodded. "We checked. Maude admitted George tried to rectify the situation when Maddie was a child. He came back every few years begging for time with her. Olivia wouldn't hear of it."

"And now?" Dwight prodded. "Last time I checked, Olivia's ghost was still hanging around. What does she have to say about all this?"

"She's surprisingly morose and petulant, which is very unlike her. She's making things difficult for Maddie."

"And how is Maddie handling that?"

"She refuses to cut George out of her life. He's been easy to get along with and goes out of his way to spend time with Maddie whenever she can spare an hour here or there. He doesn't try to dictate.

"Come to find out, he put money away for Maddie for years," he continued. "He wanted to give it to her so she could pay for the wedding, or even a honeymoon, but she turned him down. She wants to get to know her father, not be paid for the privilege."

"Most women would've assumed they were owed something in her situation."

"Maddie isn't most women."

"She's certainly not, you freak." Dwight rolled his eyes. "I hate it when you get that moony look on your face. It makes me want to smack you."

"You'll learn to live with it. I plan to whip it out for special occasions for the rest of my life."

"Yup, you're totally whipped." Dwight gestured toward Nick's phone. "Text Maddie and see if she has access to shift records. I happen to know a nurse or two who might help us so I'm going to tag them, too. If we work together, we might have a few ideas before dinner."

"That sounds like a plan to me."

ANDREA SAT AT A cubicle desk and searched personnel records, an annoyed look on her face as Maddie leaned over her shoulder.

"You're invading my personal space."

"Oh, I'm sorry." Maddie took one step back and then returned to scanning the documents over Andrea's shoulder on the computer screen. "I have a hard time seeing from back here."

"I'm sorry for that, but you're making me nervous," Andrea said. "I need to concentrate. Take a seat and watch the door."

Maddie did as instructed, although her patience was wearing thin. "Have you found anything of interest yet?"

"I don't even know where to start looking," Andrea admitted. "It's not as if I have access to private personnel records. If anyone was worried about what one of our doctors was doing, or even if complaints were filed, I wouldn't be privy to the information. They don't just leave that stuff out where anyone can see it."

"That's true." Maddie glanced down at her phone when it dinged. "Nick is texting."

"He probably can't take another moment of not being in your presence," Andrea drawled.

"I don't think that's it."

"That's because you don't always see the way he looks at you. When he thinks you're not looking, he gets this goofy look on his face while watching you. It's ridiculously pathetic and it makes me really jealous."

"Jealous?" Maddie arched an eyebrow. "Why would you be jealous?"

"Because you have the one thing everyone wants," Andrea replied. "You have a gorgeous man who is in love with you. Heck, he threw himself on top of you to protect you from a stray bullet. If that's not forever love, I don't know what is."

"Don't remind me about the bullet." Maddie wrinkled her nose as she considered the text. "Nick has a good idea."

"He does?" Andrea turned. "What's the idea?"

"I think you're right about us wasting time by searching the personnel files. Anything juicy is going to be hidden from us. That means we need to think outside the box."

"And how do you plan to do that?"

"I need to see the schedules," Maddie replied. "Like ... is there any one doctor who works a lot of late shifts?"

"I guess there would have to be," Andrea said after a beat. "Most of the doctors here don't work late hours, though. That's reserved for emergency room doctors."

"So let's look at emergency room doctors first."

"Okay. You're the boss."

"I STARTED WITH EMERGENCY ROOM DOCTORS," Dwight volunteered, turning his computer so Paloma and Nick could stare at the photos. "I know that you didn't get a really good look at the guy, but I still need you to see if you can identify anyone who looks familiar, Paloma."

The weary woman propped herself up on her elbows and stared at the photos in turn. She wrinkled her forehead in concentration, but her eyes didn't spark with a hint of recognition. After looking over the three rows of photos twice, Paloma shook her head.

"Are you saying that it isn't any of them or you simply don't know?" Nick queried.

"I don't know." Paloma's voice was thick with sleep. "I know what you want from me, but I'm not sure I can give it to you. It was dark and I only saw the edges of his face."

"Let's try something new," Nick said, pushing away the laptop and offering up a calm smile. "Why don't we start with the biggies and move to the smaller details after. What color was his hair?"

"Oh." Paloma tapped her finger on her lip. "It was dark. That's all I can say. I don't know if it was black or brown."

"That's okay." Nick was determined to be encouraging. "What about his eyes? Could you see any hint of color?"

"They were dark, too, but the whole night was dark."

"Let's talk about the shape of the eyes," Nick said. "You couldn't see the little details, but the shape is just as important. Were they round, maybe shaped like almonds? Were they big or small? What about the placement? Were they wide-set or was the space between narrow?"

Paloma screwed up her face in concentration as she thought. "Wide eyes, not close to the nose. He had one of those noses that's like a ski slope, turned up at the end. I would say his eyes were more like a circle than an oval, but I can't explain them more than that."

"No, that's good." Nick meant it. "What about a beard? Did he have any facial hair?"

"None that I saw, but he had the things." Paloma gestured to the side of her head and fluttered her fingers.

"I'm sorry, I don't know what you mean," Nick hedged.

"The things. The ... um ... hair that came down like this."

"Oh." Realization dawned. "Sideburns. He had sideburns is what you're saying."

Paloma nodded. "They were trimmed and neat but there were hints of white in them. I know because I looked hard at the side of his head right before I ran. That was the last thing I saw."

"That's very good," Dwight said, joining in the conversation. "What about anything else that stood out to you? It might not seem important, but even the smallest detail will help us. Was there anything special about his shoes? Maybe he wore cufflinks."

"What is a cufflink?" Paloma was legitimately confused.

"It's a piece of jewelry," Nick explained, holding out his arm. "When a man wears a shirt that goes underneath a suit jacket, he often uses cufflinks as sort of a decoration."

"Oh, I understand." Paloma bobbed her head. "Yes, he wore jewelry there."

"Do you remember what you saw?"

"It looked like a weird and twisty knife with wings, perhaps like angel wings."

"That sounds like the symbol for doctor," Dwight noted. "I think we're definitely on the right track."

"The only problem is that I'm guessing a lot of doctors wear that sort of cufflink."

"True."

"There was a gem in them between the wings," Paloma supplied. "It sparkled a bit when a pair of headlights hit. It was when we were walking down the street, before he frightened me. I remember thinking it was a pretty stone. Unique."

"What kind of stone?"

"It was milky, like a cloud with extra colors in it."

"That would be an opal," Nick said. "That has to cut down the list a little bit."

"I would think so," Dwight agreed. "We need to ask the nurses who wears a set of opal cufflinks. They might be able to lead us right to him."

. . .

"CRAP! I'M BEING PAGED."

Andrea glared at the device on her hip.

"What does it say?" Maddie asked, concerned.

"I have to go to the emergency ward and check on a patient," Andrea replied. "It won't take long, but I can't ignore the page."

Maddie knew that well and good. "Okay, well, I can wait here," she suggested hopefully.

Andrea let loose with a withering look. "If I leave you here, I'll probably get in big trouble."

"Not if you're quick."

Andrea heaved out a sigh. "Maddie, I don't know. I've already crossed several lines."

"I just want to look at the schedules," Maddie promised. "I won't look at anything else. If we can narrow down the schedules, at least we'll have a place to start."

"I thought we already did that. The emergency doctors are your primary focus, right?"

"Mostly. There are other doctors who moonlight in the emergency ward, though. I want to gather their names, too. If all goes as planned, I'll be completely done by the time you get back. Then no one will be the wiser when we leave."

"Oh, man." Andrea rubbed her forehead, resigned. "Fine. If I get fired for this, though, I'm moving up north to live with you. See how much romance you manage to get in with a permanent houseguest."

"I'll keep that in mind." Maddie grinned as she claimed Andrea's seat and offered up a haphazard wave. "I'll be quick. I promise."

"I won't be gone long."

"I'll be done by the time you get back. I'm almost positive."

Maddie gave the computer her full focus, pulling up the emergency room schedules so she could take a gander. Once she realized how many pages she was looking at, she opted to print them out so she could have hard copies to search later. There was no way she would be able to make it through every schedule for the past month in a short amount of time, and if she tried, that would increase the odds of her discovery.

As she waited for the papers to print, she tapped her fingers on the desktop and stared at the computer screen. She recognized some of the listed names, but she didn't know them very well. She was most often assigned to the fifth floor, which was a recovery ward. The doctors she worked with almost always stuck to that floor.

The way the computer was set up, Andrea had a virtual desktop. That meant she could keep her own items in the cloud and look at them whenever she wanted. As long as she was logged in, they were accessible. When she logged out, no one else could see them.

Most of Andrea's files were boring and mundane. Schedules, reminder lists, upcoming seminars she might be interested in. All those things were normal. One folder, though, stood out. There was no name on it, only a symbol. Maddie recognized the symbol. Half the doctors in the hospital wore it on ties, cufflinks, and even T-shirts in their off time.

Out of boredom – and even though she knew it was an invasion – Maddie double-clicked on the folder. She figured it would be something mundane but instead found herself looking at a sea of photographs. The faces all belonged to young girls and women, and they were all taken in dark places so Maddie had to strain to make out certain details. The women sat in ragged clothes and torn jackets, tears streaming down their filthy faces as they stared at the camera.

Maddie's heart skipped a beat as she flipped through the photos, dumbfounded. She had no idea what she was looking at. Then she happened upon a familiar face. It was one straight out of her nightmares.

Maddie double-clicked on the photo and when it enlarged so it was big enough to take up the entire screen, she found a terrified blond staring back. The woman was bruised and dirty, her eyes lifeless. Underneath the woman's photo was one line of text. It was a series of numbers and letters Maddie didn't recognize.

On a hunch, Maddie snapped a photograph of the text (while omitting the woman herself in case she was off base) and sent it to Nick, asking him if he knew what the numbers and letters meant. She didn't get a chance to see his return message because she was distracted by the sound of the door behind her opening.

Instinctively, Maddie closed out of the window and pulled up the schedule, hoping that whoever was behind her wasn't looking at the screen upon entry. She pasted a bright smile on her face, one that was shaky and felt fake, and turned to greet what she hoped would be a stranger or mild acquaintance. Instead she came face to face with a woman she believed up until mere seconds before to be a friend.

"That was quick."

"Yeah, it was," Andrea agreed, her face unreadable. "What were you just doing?"

Uh-oh. Maddie knew she was in trouble now. "I was just looking at the schedules. In fact, I think I found what I was looking for." She got to her feet, her heart skipping a beat when Andrea tensed. "I can't thank you enough for helping me. You always were a great friend. I have to get going, though."

Andrea's sigh was weary and worn. "Yeah, we both know that's not going to happen. Sit down, Maddie. I think we need to have a talk."

18. EIGHTEEN

Maddie's heart thumped hard as she tried to maintain control of her emotions.

"I just need to run and talk to Nick." Her voice sounded unnaturally squeaky, but she had trouble controlling it. "We can talk when I get back."

Andrea moved to cut off Maddie's avenue of escape. "I don't think that's a good idea."

"Uh-huh. Well ... ." Maddie clutched her phone in her hand, the instinct to call Nick overwhelming. Of course, she was under no delusion that she would be able to do that with Andrea watching her. The woman wasn't overly large, but she was strong enough to put up a fight. Since Maddie had no way to escape, she figured keeping her distance from Andrea was the smarter way to go. "I should call Nick."

"Don't even think about it." Andrea extended a warning finger, all traces of warmth and consideration absent from her face. "You don't want to make this worse than it already is."

Maddie had no idea if that was even possible. "I don't understand why you're so aggressive all of a sudden," she lied, hoping she could pull off an innocent act that was so profound Andrea would have no choice but to believe her. "I just want to talk to Nick. It's not a big deal."

"Right, you just want to talk to your tall slab of beefcake," Andrea drawled, rolling her eyes. "Do you really think I'm going to fall for that?"

Maddie's mind was racing. "I don't know why you're being like this."

"Really? Do you think I'm stupid?" Andrea flexed her hands into fists. "Don't play games with me, Maddie. We both know what you saw. I didn't realize until I was halfway down to the emergency room that you would probably stumble across the file. You always were a busybody."

Maddie balked. "I'm not a busybody. I've never been a busybody."

"You've always been a busybody," Andrea shot back. "You've gotten away with it until now because of the way you look, but you've always been up in everybody's business even though people choose to look the other way. I mean ... when people look at you they see an angel. When people look at me they see the angel's ugly sister."

Maddie's mouth dropped open. "That's not true."

"Oh, it's true." Andrea was almost ranting as she paced in front of the door. "All I ever wanted was to find a nice doctor and settle down. That's why I became a nurse. I knew I wouldn't get one of the younger doctors, one of the hotshots, and I was okay with that. I don't look like a model, after all, but I'm hardly deformed or anything. Doctors like everyone wants, hot doctors, are reserved for women like you."

Maddie had no idea where this conversation was going, but she was massively uncomfortable with it all the same. "I think you're being too hard on yourself."

"It hardly matters," Andrea continued. She was talking to herself more than Maddie at this point. "I knew coming in what my options would be. Imagine my surprise, though, when even the older doctors were focused on you."

Maddie was dumbfounded. "That never happened."

"It *did* happen. It did! I was open for offers and even suggested a few outings myself. No one paid me a lick of attention because you were here. All they could talk about was you."

"That's not exactly how I remember things."

"Oh, you wouldn't." Andrea's tone was practically dripping with sarcasm. "You were above it all. You were oblivious to all the attention you garnered. You didn't have a clue that they all wanted you and no one wanted me.

"Quite frankly, the happiest day of my life was when you put in your two weeks' notice," she continued. "As soon as you were out of the building things got better for me. Oh, sure, there was some mourning and lamenting of your departure. There were even some people who thought you would return and they held out hope for a long time.

"Me, though, I was thrilled you were gone and I knew you wouldn't come back because you were never happy here," she said. "Everyone else missed that little detail, but I knew you were miserable and it made me glad because the one thing you couldn't magically snap your fingers and get was apparently happiness."

Maddie had no idea what to say. "So basically you think I'm to blame for everything bad that's ever happened to you, huh?"

"Not everything. Just the stuff that's happened since I met you."

"Well, that sounds like a healthy attitude," Maddie snarked. "It's not at all ridiculous or immature."

Andrea narrowed her eyes to dangerous slits. "I would be very careful how you talk to me," she threatened. "In case you haven't noticed, I'm the one in charge here. Me!" She thumped her chest for emphasis, the sound offering up a hollow echo in the deserted room. "You're going to do what I want for a change."

Maddie licked her lips as she internally debated her options. "And how do you think that's going to work? All I have to do is scream. Once I do, you're done."

"Really? Do you think so? You're in a restricted area. Go ahead and scream. They'll believe me when I tell them you snuck in without authorization. I dare you to scream."

Andrea sounded sure of herself, but Maddie knew better. She recognized insecurity and worry when she saw it.

"I don't really care if they believe me or you. I simply want to make sure that you don't do something you're going to regret."

"I regret nothing."

Maddie decided to approach the problem head-on. "Nothing? You don't regret having a hand in the death of at least twenty girls. That somehow seems wrong."

Andrea puckered her mouth but didn't immediately respond.

"I'm serious," Maddie pressed. "What were you thinking? How could you be involved in this?"

"You don't even know what you're talking about," Andrea complained. "You don't even know what this is."

"It's killing ... on a massive scale."

"It's cleaning," Andrea corrected. "We're cleaning up the neighborhood."

We're? Maddie realized relatively quickly that Andrea couldn't possibly be working alone. It made no sense otherwise. Of course she had a partner. Paloma said a man approached her. A man's strength would be necessary to carry a body. The twist wasn't that Andrea had a partner. No, actually the twist was that the man they were all looking for from the beginning had a partner ... and she just happened to be female.

"You're cleaning it up? How?"

"Have you looked around, Maddie?" Andrea sounded weary. "This place is a cesspool. There are illegals running around taking things they shouldn't be taking. There are women peddling sex for money. There are drugs being sold on every corner. We're trying to eradicate all of that."

The answer didn't make sense to Maddie. "If you're going after the dregs on equal footing, how come all of your victims have been women?"

"I ... ." Andrea worked her jaw.

"Because you don't pick the victims," Maddie surmised. "Your partner does. Who is he?"

"I'm not at liberty to say." Andrea's tone was cool and clipped. "It doesn't matter. We're doing a good thing for the neighborhood. Once it's clean and the bad element is gone, we'll be able to refurbish the buildings ... bring new people to the area. It will allow for economic recovery. Isn't that what we all want?"

"That sounds very well-rehearsed. I don't believe it for a second, though."

"You need you to get on board with this, Maddie. If you don't, it won't end well for you."

Even though she was keen on staying alive, Maddie had no intention of pretending to be anything other than what she was. "Why would I possibly get on board with this? You're killing people."

"I never killed anyone." Andrea was matter-of-fact. "I simply helped in the background."

"Do you think that makes you innocent?"

"No, but I don't feel an ounce of guilt so if that's where you're going with this conversation, I would direct it elsewhere. There's nothing you can say that will make me change my mind. We did the right thing."

"So ... how did it work? Convince me."

"It wasn't an especially deep operation," Andrea replied, leaning her hip against one of the cubicles nearest the door. "We identified individuals who were bringing down the neighborhood and we eradicated them."

"How?"

"What do you mean?"

"How did you eradicate them?" Maddie pressed. "Did you shoot them? Strangle them? Stab them?"

"Aren't you friends with the detective in charge? Shouldn't you already know that?"

Maddie racked her brain. Dwight hadn't been forthcoming with any of the details, but she knew a few of them from the visions she had. "I know your friend used a knife at least two or three times. Some of the bodies were chopped up, too, so I'm guessing he used bigger tools when it warranted."

"Chopped up?" Andrea furrowed her brow. "Why would they be chopped up?"

It was only then that Maddie realized Andrea was so far in the dark she would need her own moon to get out. "You really have no idea what's going on, do you?"

"I told you. We're cleaning up the neighborhood."

"That might've been what your partner told you, but that's not what was going on. You weren't cleaning up the neighborhood. You were enabling a hunter."

Andrea snorted. "Don't be absurd. It was a cleanup effort. We talked about it for weeks before we started."

"Yes, but how many trips were you present for?" Maddie challenged. "Whoever you're working with needed the occasional alibi, I'm going to guess. That's why he involved you. You also made a convenient scapegoat. If he got caught, he could point the finger at you. In fact, I'm going to guess, that when the police raid his stronghold – wherever that may be – he'll have a ton of evidence that implicates you and nothing that points to himself."

Andrea balked. "You have no idea what you're talking about. The person I'm working with, the person I'm going to spend the rest of my life with, would never do anything of the sort. Oh, yes, I can see you're confused. That's the part of the story you're missing, Maddie. I finally found my doctor."

"He just happens to be a homicidal maniac," Maddie gritted out, squeezing her phone. She wanted to call Nick more than anything but couldn't figure out a way to make it work without tipping off Andrea. "How could you do this? You're a nurse, for crying out loud. You're supposed to want to help those in need, not hurt them."

"Only the right sort of people," Andrea corrected. "You can't have a healthy society when certain people are dragging it down. It's a harsh lesson to learn, but once you learn it things will get easier. You have to accept that certain people are limited."

"Funnily enough, I was thinking the exact same thing," Maddie said. "Ultimately it doesn't matter, though. This little operation is done."

"And how do you figure that?"

"Because I won't play your game." Maddie lifted her phone and hit the keypad. "You're done. It's over. You need to accept that."

"What do you think you're doing?" Andrea leaned forward, alarmed. "Who do you think you're calling?"

"I'm calling Nick. I'm done listening to your nonsense. This entire thing has to stop."

"And you think I'm going to let you stop it?"

"I don't think you have a choice."

"Think again!"

Andrea moved quickly, circling the first row of cubicles and launching herself at Maddie. Maddie barely had a chance to hit the button that would allow her to connect with Nick before she found herself flying backward.

Maddie hit the ground hard, oxygen being forced from her lungs. She needed a moment to recover, but she didn't have it because Andrea's hands were wrapping around her neck to cut off the flow of oxygen. Maddie tried to buck off the woman, but Andrea had the leverage and she wasn't afraid to use it.

"You have to ruin absolutely everything!" Andrea screeched. "Why won't you just stay out of my life?"

"WELL, I GOT THE schedule and there are two things I find to be odd," Dwight said, shifting his laptop so Nick could see the screen. "We don't have dates for when the women were taken ... er, at least not a complete set of dates. All we know is that some women went missing from the streets, but we have no timetable.

"Several of the women taken – two of them were identified first because they had records on file – weren't like the others," he continued. "One, Barb Norris, was a student at Wayne State University. She was taking science classes, but she volunteered her time here."

Nick cocked an eyebrow. "Here? As in the hospital?"

Dwight nodded. "She took three shifts a week. Apparently she was considering being a nurse. Her roommate reported her missing the first night after she didn't come home, although she wasn't allowed to file a formal complaint until twenty-four hours later. The time of the initial complaint is clearly marked, though."

"So she worked here," Nick mused, rubbing his chin. "That's another tie."

"Yes, and Adrienne Kennedy is one of the other women we identified right away," Dwight said. "She was also a student, young and pretty. She worked twenty hours a week in the cafeteria."

"At the school?"

Dwight shook his head. "Here at the hospital."

"And there's your other thread," Nick said. "We wondered why those two women were so vastly different from the rest. They were low risk, which never made sense."

"They both disappeared after late shifts here," Dwight said. "That's on top of Tessa Roth, who was also identified early and actually worked here. I don't know why I didn't see it or notice it before. Perhaps I wasn't looking hard enough because the idea of it being a doctor seemed so ridiculous."

"Okay, that's somewhere to start," Nick noted. "Can we cross-reference staff workers who had late shifts on those days?"

"I was just starting that when I got an immediate hit," Dwight said. "Ironically, it's someone you already dislike."

Nick was practically salivating. "Who?" His phone picked that moment to go off. "Hold on a second, I think Maddie is calling." He lifted the device to his ear. "What's up, love?"

MADDIE GROWLED AS SHE tried to fight off Andrea's maniacal efforts to kill her. Oxygen was in short supply but Maddie managed a quick inhalation when Andrea shifted her hands.

"I hate you!" Andrea screeched. "You have no idea how much I hate you. You always have to ruin everything. That's simply what you do.

"Do you have any idea how good my life was going before you showed up?" she continued, her eyes madly flitting back and forth. "Things were perfect and now you want to ruin them. You almost ruined them the first time by stealing his attention. Once you left, though, he let it go. Now you're back and you're going to ruin things all over again!"

Maddie dug her fingernails into Andrea's wrists as hard as she could, causing the woman to cry out. Maddie bucked her narrow hips at the exact moment, causing Andrea to careen to the side and smack her head into the nearest cubicle.

Maddie took advantage of Andrea's momentary confusion and managed to wriggle away from the demented woman in the intervening seconds, lashing out with her foot and making contact with Andrea's ribs in her attempt to escape.

Because she was shaky, Maddie opted to crawl rather than immediately get to her feet. She was five feet away when she realized someone else had entered the room. She rolled to her side and focused on the familiar face.

"Call for help! She's crazy. She's one of the murderers."

The doctor – and he was a doctor – merely shook his head as he tsked. "Well, this isn't good. I told you to take care of her quietly, Andrea. How do you think we're going to make this go away?"

Maddie sucked in a breath when she realized Andrea's partner had joined the party and she was in even more trouble than before.

"I guess I should've known it was you."

"Yes, well, we can both agree about that. You need to learn to think things out before acting. Alas, I think it's too late for that to turn into an acquired skill for you."

19. NINETEEN

Nick was confused as he glanced at his phone.

"Hello?"

The only response on the other end of the call was muted noise and a girly trill of sorts that Nick was sure came from Maddie.

"Hello?"

"What is it?" Dwight asked, instantly alert.

"I don't know." Nick stared at his phone for a long beat. "I don't hear anything."

"Maybe it's just a dropped call."

"Maybe." Nick had trouble believing that. "I ... ." He broke off when he heard whispering, a soft kiss against his ear that he was sure no one else would hear. He didn't recognize the voice at first but realized it was Olivia fairly quickly. Her message was clear. Panic licked his spine and the hair on the back of his neck stood on end. "Maddie is in trouble."

Dwight's eyebrows flew up his forehead. "How can you possibly know that?"

"I just know." Nick was firm. "Maddie is in trouble and needs me. We have to find whatever room Andrea took her to."

"Because Andrea is going to hurt her?"

"I ... don't know. I just know that Maddie is in trouble."

"I hate to ask but ... how can you know that?" Dwight wasn't interested in fighting Nick, but the shift in the man's demeanor was enough to set his teeth on edge.

"Let's just say a little birdie told me," Nick suggested, risking a glance over his shoulder and finding nothing staring back. The whispering had ceased, but his determination was set. "We need to find Maddie right now. Whatever is happening, it most certainly isn't all right."

"Then let's find her."

"Wait." Nick grabbed Dwight's arm before he could stroll out of the room. "Who were you about to tell me about? Who is the doctor?"

"It's funny you should ask."

MADDIE RUEFULLY RUBBED her cheek as she stared at Milton Tipton. His expression was hard to read as he stood in the doorway and surveyed the scene in front of him.

In truth, Maddie was angry at herself for not figuring it out sooner. Tipton was a fussy know-it-all who thought he was smarter than everyone else in the room. Doctors had to clean their hands multiple times a day for sanitary reasons, but he was almost brutal about the process, scrubbing twice as long and dumping whatever chemicals he could find on his hands, something that always got the nurses talking about possible OCD.

He was also politically minded. Maddie remembered hearing him discuss politics in various break rooms around the hospital, although it was never a normal political discussion. It wasn't about being a Democrat or Republican as much as it was about social ideals that never seemed to make a lot of sense.

In hindsight, Maddie realized he was the easy answer and she shied away from suggesting him because of that. She should've gone with her instincts, although it was far too late to change things.

"What is going on here, Andrea?" Tipton's voice was harsh and clipped. Maddie could see people bustling about the hospital on the other side of the door, which gave her hope, but she knew she was in quite the pickle all the same. Now she was outnumbered and separated from the door by two bodies "Do you realize what sort of position you've put me in?"

Andrea, who was busy rubbing her head and staring with wide-eyed astonishment, seemed to be having trouble wrapping her brain around what was happening. "I ... you ... I ... um ... ."

"Yes, well, I see your astounding conversational skills remain intact," Tipton said derisively, making a disappointed sound with his tongue. "I really cannot believe you did this. Have you no sense at all?"

Since she wasn't sure what to do with the new information, Maddie was completely comfortable letting Tipton and Andrea duke it out while she formulated a plan. In fact, if Tipton and Andrea forgot she was even in the room, she was convinced that would be the best possible outcome.

Alas, that was not in the cards.

"This isn't my fault," Andrea whined, adopting a pitiable look. "She pushed things too far and stuck her nose where it didn't belong."

"And who put herself in this position to begin with?" Tipton sounded as if he was talking to a child rather than a girlfriend.

"It wasn't my fault." Andrea made a face. "I don't see why you're blaming me."

"Yes, well, we'll talk about that in a little bit." Tipton leveled his gaze on Maddie and it took everything she had inside for the frightened blond to maintain her footing in the face of his chilly glare. "It seems we've found ourselves in a bit of a predicament."

"I would say so." Maddie refused to cower in front of the man so she squared her shoulders. "You're a killer and you enlisted Andrea to help you with the dirty work of your operation. That's definitely a predicament."

"That's a pedestrian answer," Tipton countered. "I'm not a killer. I'm a cleaner."

"I think that's simply a nice word you want to use because it makes it easier to justify your actions," Maddie supplied. "You're a killer. You're a predator. I know what you did to those women."

"And what's that?"

"You hunted them."

Tipton's brow wrinkled. "I don't think you understand the nature of my operation. I didn't go into this as a means to hurt people. That's simply a byproduct. In the end, the community will be better off because of my efforts."

"Really?" Maddie's stomach twisted. He appeared so rational that she had trouble reconciling the man who stood before her with the things she knew he did. "If that's true, why did you get off on the hunt? Why did you chase them through alleys? Why did you catch some of them and let them go only so you could chase them again?"

Tipton balked, surprise over Maddie's profound knowledge throwing him for a loop. "I don't know what you mean."

Andrea shot Tipton a quizzical look, confused. "That didn't happen."

"It *did* happen," Maddie argued. "He hunted the women he took." She searched her memory for an important scene from the vision. "In fact, there was one woman – she had long auburn hair, although I think it was a wig because the hair was clearly acrylic – and he took her to an abandoned building.

"I'm not sure what building, but I know he made it so the doors were locked from the outside and she had no way to get out," she continued. "He let her loose on the top floor and then proceeded to hunt her through the building. I think it might've been a former department store. Maybe one of those old, dilapidated buildings down on Woodward."

Tipton's face turned ashen. "How can you possibly know that?"

Andrea's voice turned shrill. "It's true? You never told me that. Why wouldn't you tell me? We're supposed to be a couple. I told you what my therapist said. She said if we expect to make it for the long haul, we have to communicate with one another."

Tipton ignored Andrea's outburst. "I'm really curious how you know about that, Ms. Graves. The woman's name was Sherry, by the way. She was a prostitute who locked her ten-year-old son in her apartment while she went out and turned tricks. Are you honestly saying she was worth saving?"

Maddie shrugged, refusing to engage in a moral argument with a man who clearly didn't possess empathy. "I don't think it's my place to judge others. I don't know the woman in question. I do know that she was terrified, that you wore her down when you chased her through the building.

"I also know that you taunted her from the darkness," she continued. "You had a knife and you showed it to her and you kept letting her get away. You played with her until she was so terrified, so afraid, it was almost a relief for her when it was over.

"Her last thought was of her son, though," Maddie said, absently scratching at the side of her nose as she absorbed the vision for a second time. "She was sorry because she worried he would never know what happened to her. She didn't want him to think she'd simply walked away and didn't love him."

"Oh, well, that's a pretty story," Tipton sneered. "You're clearly making it up, though."

"If that's what you want to believe, I can't stop you." Now it was Maddie's turn to be matter-of-fact. "That's not how things went down, though."

Tipton stared at Maddie a long beat, his mind racing. Out of nowhere, he shifted his stance and held out his hands in a placating manner. "I don't think you understand what I was trying to do. If you understood, if things were better explained, you would be open to the outcome. You must understand ... things are getting better."

"I'll never be open to what you're suggesting."

"I think you're wrong." Tipton offered up a smile that was without mirth or warmth. "I think you're simply missing the bigger picture. When I tell you why ... when I explain how much better things are ... you'll come around to my way of thinking. In fact, I think you might want to join the team."

Maddie barely managed to bite back her distaste. "You think I'll want to join the team? Your team? Why would I possibly want that?"

"Why would you possibly want that?" Andrea challenged, regaining her senses as she stared at her partner. "Why do you care if Maddie gets with the program?"

"I don't care," Tipton replied. "I simply hate for people to live in ignorance."

"And is that what you think she's doing?" Andrea asked. "I mean ... do you think she's stupid? Is that the issue here?"

"I didn't say she was stupid," Tipton clarified. "I hardly think that. She was one of the better nurses we've had on staff at this facility. That hardly makes her stupid."

"She left, though," Andrea reminded him. "She couldn't wait to get out of here, to get away from you."

Tipton narrowed his eyes. "That's not exactly how I remember things going."

"Then you're remembering wrong."

Maddie bit the inside of her cheek as she watched the interplay. She couldn't understand how the conversation had managed to take such a turn. Even more than that, though, she didn't fully grasp the dynamic between the players. She was starting to get the feeling that Tipton would rather cut Andrea's throat than be what the woman yearned for him to be. Maddie figured she could work with that if the opportunity arose.

"And what am I remembering wrong?" Tipton asked. "I seem to recall Ms. Graves having to leave because her mother died. She had no other choice. The story included something about a grandmother who was old and suffering from ill health. Most everyone believed Ms. Graves would return once her grandmother shuffled off the mortal coil."

Maddie was flabbergasted. "What? How can you possibly say something like that?"

Tipton didn't answer, instead remaining focused on Andrea. "You shouldn't talk out of turn. We've discussed this. If you don't have the appropriate answer, then you shouldn't try intercepting the question."

"Oh, whatever." Andrea's face twisted as she pulled herself to a standing position and dusted off the seat of her scrubs. "You don't think I know what's going on here, but I know everything that's going on. I understand what you're doing. I'm not an idiot."

Tipton crossed his arms over his chest, giving Maddie a clear view of his hands. He didn't appear to be armed. Of course, that didn't mean he didn't have a weapon of some sort – a scalpel maybe – in the pocket of his coat. She would have to be careful.

"I didn't say you were an idiot," Tipton said evenly. "If you heard that, perhaps you should clean your ears."

Andrea wasn't even remotely mollified. "You might not have said it, but you're thinking it."

"Oh, well, thinking it is entirely different. I'm definitely thinking it."

Andrea's mouth dropped open. "What?"

"You heard me." Tipton looked as if he were at the end of his rope. "I don't want to keep going around with you. This fight between us – this ridiculous little spat – is not helpful and, frankly, it's a waste of time."

"You think my feelings are a waste of time?"

"I think most feelings are a waste of time," Tipton replied. "Now, try to be a good girl for a few minutes." He lifted his finger to his lips to offer up an admonishment for silence. "I need to talk to Ms. Graves. It's important that we get her on our side because, if we don't, we're going to have some tough decisions to make."

Andrea was incredulous. "Why not just kill her right here?"

Maddie's heart skipped a beat. "If you're taking votes, I'm going to cast mine against that option."

Tipton and Andrea remained focused on each other rather than Maddie, seemingly oblivious that she'd even spoken.

"Well, let's think about that in a reasonable manner," Tipton drawled. He was back to using his "teacher" voice, although he didn't sound as if he had a lot of patience for his student. "If we kill Ms. Graves here, how do you think we'll get away with it?"

"We'll just walk away and pretend we don't know anything about it."

"Uh-huh. And since we both had to swipe our access cards to enter, how is that going to work?"

"Oh. I didn't think of that." Andrea pressed the heel of her hand to her forehead. "Well, we can kill her and carry her out."

Tipton gestured toward the door. "Have you looked around out there? I think one of the fifty people hanging around in the lobby might notice if we start carrying around a body."

It was as if they were talking about scheduling grocery shopping for the week, Maddie realized. They were both so far gone they couldn't see the crazy writing on the wall. She took advantage of their distraction to start typing on her phone. They didn't so much as glance in her direction.

"So we'll kill her in here, stuff her body in one of the cubicles, and come back for it later when the night shift comes on," Andrea suggested. "You know they're not very observant."

"And what happens when someone comes in to use the computers and stumbles over a dead body?" Tipton challenged, exasperation evident.

"We'll put a sign on the door," Andrea said, her eyes lighting up. "We'll grab one of those 'out of order' signs from the bathroom and put it on the door. No one will dare enter."

"Right, because no one ignores those signs," Tipton drawled. "Good grief, Andrea. You need to get a grip."

Tipton rolled his neck and stared at the ceiling. "We have no choice but to move her out of this room while she's still alive. That will give us time to confine her in one of my buildings until she sees the light and joins us."

Andrea immediately started shaking her head. "Do you really think I'm going to agree to that? You're an absolute imbecile if you think that's going to happen."

"Please. I have an IQ of 180."

"That doesn't mean you're not an imbecile."

"I hardly think you're the one to judge when it comes to being an imbecile," Tipton said, causing Andrea's eyes to fire.

"I knew you were going to do this," Andrea snapped. "I knew the second Maddie walked back into this hospital that you were going to turn on me. I saw it on your face when you first saw her. You didn't know I was there, did you? I saw you hiding in the shadows, though. I saw the look on your face when you saw Nick. You were disappointed and jealous. Yeah, I said it. You were jealous of Nick. Everyone saw it."

"Is that his name?" Tipton's tone was mild, as if he was mostly disinterested in the conversation. "I don't care about him either way. I merely said that I couldn't understand how Ms. Graves ended up with a man of his ... limited ... intellectual range."

Maddie didn't want to draw attention to herself, but she was offended on Nick's behalf. She opened her mouth to say something snide and then thought better of it and returned to her texting. She was a good fifteen feet away from Tipton and Andrea and neither one of them made a move to head in her direction. As long as things remained that way, Maddie knew she could organize her own rescue.

"Yeah, but what you were really saying is you couldn't understand how she could want Nick and not you," Andrea spat. "You might not have said the words, but you're not good at hiding your intent. I've always been able to read you."

"Is that so?" Tipton didn't look convinced. "I have a hard time believing that."

"You have a hard time believing anything that you didn't come up with yourself," Andrea shot back. "I know, though. I know everything you did when Maddie was still in town. I know that you sat outside her apartment building until the early hours of the morning hoping for a glimpse of her in her windows."

Maddie's head jerked up as she snapped her eyes to Tipton. "What?"

"Oh, you didn't know that?" Andrea snorted, clearly enjoying herself. "It's true. He used to follow you home from your shifts and watch you from the streets. I know because I was following him."

"That seems a bit stalkerish," Maddie noted. "Actually, it's a bit weird on both your parts."

"I knew what I wanted and I was determined to get it," Andrea argued. "I wanted a doctor and I knew Milton here was my best shot.

He made a lot of money and had a personality no one could love, which meant I was probably his only option.

"My only problem was getting him to notice me when you were around," she continued. "He didn't even know I was alive when he was following you around. I was considering killing you myself when you announced you were leaving. It was as if you read my mind the day you told me because I had big plans for following you home myself one night."

A chill went through Maddie's body. "I see."

"I still considered following you to Blackstone Bay and handling things even after," Andrea admitted. "I thought he wasn't going to let go of you – he even went to your apartment right after your last shift here, if you can believe that – but he only pouted for a few weeks before regrouping."

Something horrifying occurred to Maddie. "Regrouping?" She fixed her eyes on Tipton. "Did you regroup by coming up with your cleaning plan?"

Tipton pursed his lips and shrugged, delight flickering through his eyes. "I might have. It was just an idea at first, you have to understand. If I didn't have so much time on my hands without you to pursue, I don't think the idea would've presented itself. I really have you to thank."

Maddie thought she might throw up. "I really hope that isn't true."

"But it is." Tipton's smile was benign. "I owe everything I am to you."

Maddie stared at him for a long time, blinking twice in slow succession before speaking. "I don't want credit for you being a sadistic freak. I don't want to be a part of any of this."

"You'll change your mind once we have some time together," Tipton argued. "You'll come around to my way of thinking."

"Do you really believe that?"

"I do." Tipton bobbed his head, seemingly oblivious to the nonsense he spouted. "I've thought a lot about you over the years – both when you were here and when you weren't – and I knew you would eventually return. When you came back, I wanted a safe place for you to call home. I did all of this for you."

"Don't even say that!" Maddie snapped, taking everyone – including herself – by surprise with her vehemence. "You didn't do this for me. You're using me as a symbol, but you didn't do this for me.

"You did this for you," she continued, working overtime to keep from bursting into tears thanks to the frustration threatening to overwhelm her. "You did this because you liked doing it. As for you, Andrea, you did it to get ahead in the world. You knew he was a monster and yet you didn't care. You're almost worse than him because he's sick enough in the head to convince himself of things that couldn't possibly be true. You know better and yet you simply don't care."

"Why would I care?" Andrea was back to being aggressive. "Why would I possibly care about any of those women? They were nothing. They couldn't offer anything to anyone. The world is better without them."

"Maybe that's what people will say about you when you're in prison," Maddie suggested.

"Oh, I'm not going to prison," Andrea said. "I'm going to kill you before that's even a possibility."

"You're not going to kill her," Tipton snapped. "I'm bringing her onboard. Eventually she's going to be a member of our team."

"No! That's not going to happen." Andrea stomped her foot on the cold linoleum. "I won't allow it to happen. You want to bring her on and displace me and I simply won't allow it!"

Tipton let loose with a long-suffering sigh. "I think you're being unreasonable."

"And I think you're back to being a moron," Andrea shot back.

Maddie could do nothing but shake her head as the door to the room burst open and allowed Nick and Dwight entrance. They weren't alone, several of Dwight's uniformed officers trailed behind, and the looks on Tipton and Andrea's faces when they realized they were about to be overrun were almost comical.

"You," Tipton hissed, his eyes searing into Maddie's soul as she glared at her. "You did this. You told them where we were."

"Did you really think I wouldn't?" Maddie asked, remaining rooted to her spot as Dwight grabbed Tipton by the shoulders and slammed him against a cubicle.

"Keep your hands where I can see them," Dwight ordered.

"This is not my fault!" Andrea screeched as two officers grappled with her arms and wrestled her to the ground. "I didn't do this. I'm not guilty. He forced me to participate if I wanted to stay alive. I want a deal!"

"You cretin," Tipton shot back. "Don't even think of turning on me. You won't like what happens if you even consider doing that."

Nick swooped in and tugged Maddie into his arms, pressing a kiss to her cheek as he hugged her. "You scared me, love."

"I was scared, too," Maddie admitted. "At least at first. I wasn't scared so much after ... just disgusted and sad. They didn't even see me texting you."

"Well, it was helpful that you could give us a picture of the room." Nick pushed Maddie's hair away from her face. "Are you sure you're okay?"

Maddie nodded as she rested her head on his chest. "I'm okay. I'm sick to my stomach over what they did, but I'm okay."

"Good." Nick kissed the top of her head. "I love you, Maddie."

"I love you, too."

20. TWENTY

Nick brought Maddie a bottle of water and sat next to her on a couch as Dwight and his officers dealt with Tipton and Andrea. For their part, both halves of the guilty party seemed eager to point the finger at each other.

"He did it." Andrea was adamant, her hands cuffed behind her back. "He's the one who did all of it and he forced me to cover for him by threatening to kill me. I'm the wronged party."

"She's lying." Tipton managed to remain calm despite the circumstances. "She's the one who did all of it. I've suspected her for some time and I've been amassing evidence to prove her guilt. If you go to my house and look in the office you'll find everything you need to exonerate me and lock her up forever."

Dwight, who looked weary and yet relieved, dragged a hand through his hair as he glanced between faces. "Uh-huh." He turned his eyes to Maddie. "What do you have to say about all of this?"

"They're both guilty," Maddie answered without hesitation, ignoring the pleading look that crossed Tipton's face. "They admitted it. They were debating about killing me versus kidnapping me and locking me up until they could turn me to their way of thinking when you guys came in. I recorded a lot of their conversation on my phone in between texting you messages."

"I'm going to need those recordings," Dwight said.

Maddie nodded. "I understand."

The look on Tipton's face was one of irritation rather than remorse. "I'm disappointed in you, Ms. Graves."

"Coming from you I'll take that as a compliment," Maddie said. "If you were proud of me there would definitely be something wrong."

"Oh, he was never proud of you," Andrea spat. "You were never anything more than a pretty woman to parade around. Don't think that he ever thought more of you than that."

Maddie stared Andrea down for a long beat. "I never wanted to be anything to him. I think you're getting me confused with you."

"And I think you're so full of yourself I'm thankful I'm going to jail so I don't have to look at you again," Andrea shot back. "You ruined my life, by the way. I hope you know that."

"Now that right there is something I'm proud of," Maddie said.

Nick slipped his arm around her shoulders and moved his hand to the back of her neck. He could feel the tension pooling there and was unsure how to soothe her frazzled nerves. "You don't have to sit here for this, love." He kept his voice low. "We can go back to the hotel if you want."

Maddie shook her head. "I want to give my statement now. I don't want to drag it out."

Nick remained leery of letting Maddie plow forward but he ultimately nodded. "Okay. We'll finish it up now."

"Then I want to go home tomorrow," Maddie added. "First thing, right after breakfast. I'm ready to be done with the city."

Dwight, who was sidling closer, offered up a sympathetic look. "I'm sorry, Maddie. This is all my fault."

Maddie balked. "How do you figure that? You didn't kill those girls. You didn't think you were on some mission to clean the city."

"No, but I was the one who called you here. I'm the reason you got shot at by a pimp who was trying to scare his former employee – we picked him up about an hour ago, by the way, I just got a text while we were sorting through this so that's one less thing to worry about.

You would've been happier had I left you alone in Blackstone Bay. I promised you wouldn't be in danger and yet that's how things ended up ... again. I don't blame you if you're angry."

"I'm not angry with you, Dwight." Maddie opted for honesty. "I'm angry at the situation. I'm angry about what they said ... and what they did ... and how I was at the center of all of it."

Nick shifted on his seat, curious and concerned. "What do you mean by that?"

Maddie launched into the tale, occasionally glancing at Dwight who took copious notes. She refused to look at Andrea and Tipton, who the uniformed officers kept close to the nurses' station as they listened, and laid everything out. She told them about Tipton stalking her when she lived in the city, even though she didn't realize it at the time. She told them about his plan to clean up the surrounding neighborhoods and lure her back after Maude died, which still seemed ridiculous. She told them about how Tipton hunted the women.

When she was done, she felt lighter. "They're both sick. They're the sort of people who shouldn't be in this world."

"Definitely." Dwight gave Maddie's hand a squeeze before glancing over his shoulder. "I'm willing to bet you weren't the only one Dr. Tipton stalked, though. Don't take all this on yourself. It's unnecessary and a total waste of time."

Maddie was understandably puzzled. "What do you mean?"

Dwight explained what he and Nick discovered during Maddie's absence, about the three women who had ties to the hospital.

"He wasn't cleaning up the neighborhood when he went after them," Dwight supplied. "I'm guessing they turned down his advances and that's why he selected them. He was hardly the crusader he pretended to be."

Andrea darted a set of suspicious eyes to Tipton. "The girl from the cafeteria. She was one of them, wasn't she?"

Tipton averted his gaze. "I want a lawyer." His efforts to gain sympathy from the cops were clearly over. "I'm not speaking again until I have a lawyer."

"Oh, don't worry. I don't think we're going to need you." Dwight offered up a grimace to Andrea. "I think we're going to have an easy time getting all our answers."

"She's a liar, though," Tipton said. "She won't tell the truth. She's too stupid to understand the truth. She never grasped any of it."

"Oh, shut up," Andrea snapped. "You're not nearly as smart as you think you are." She turned so she was facing Dwight. "I'll answer whatever you want. Put a deal in front of me and I'll sign it. I'm so sick of this whole thing you have no idea."

Dwight grunted in reply. "Yes, it's all about you." He made a disgusted sound in the back of his throat before swiveling back to Maddie. "This wasn't all about you, Maddie, no matter what they said. It's important you know that."

Nick recognized the guilt coursing through the man, and while he wasn't thrilled with how things went down, he knew that carrying unnecessary blame wouldn't be good for Dwight or Maddie. "It's no one's fault," he offered. "Er, well, it's no one's fault but those two." He jerked his head in Andrea and Tipton's general direction. "They did this."

"They had a lot of reasons for doing it," Maddie pointed out. "They might not have been good reasons, but they were reasons all the same."

Nick cupped Maddie's chin and forced her eyes to him. "They had excuses, love. They didn't have reasons. You know that, right?"

Maddie thought about arguing, but she was too tired. In truth, she did grasp that whatever rationales Andrea and Tipton tossed in her direction were nothing more than empty diversions. "I know." She wrapped her fingers around Nick's wrist. "I know it's not my fault. I can't help but feel a little guilty because he said it only happened because I left, but I know it's not my fault."

"Mad, he was going to do something like this no matter what." Nick pressed his forehead to hers. "He's wired wrong in the head. He's not a good person and he's trying to put this on you so he can make himself look better. This is not your fault."

"I know." Maddie mostly meant it. Even though she was involved with Paloma and what happened to her, even though she was determined to help her if possible, she was ready to put the rest of it behind her. "I'm tired, though. I'm ready to go home."

"Me, too." Nick pressed a quick kiss to the corner of her mouth and then drew her to her feet. "We're going back to the hotel, Dwight. We're leaving after breakfast tomorrow. If you have questions before then ... ."

"I'll probably have questions, but I'll meet you guys for breakfast." Dwight offered up a half-hearted smile. "You guys definitely need some rest. Also, um, you know you're probably going to have to come back to testify, right? You can't completely say goodbye to the city no matter what you want."

"I know." Maddie's voice was small but strong. "I don't mind visiting, especially since you're here. I'm glad I don't live here any longer, though."

"That makes two of us." Nick wrapped his arm around her waist. "Things worked out how they were supposed to, love. Sometimes fate steps in to solve problems, and that's what happened here.

"You belong with me in Blackstone Bay, but we can visit the city occasionally," he continued. "You never belonged here, though."

"No, I didn't." Maddie glanced around the hospital, seemingly with new eyes. "I definitely ended up where I was supposed to be ... and with the one person who makes everything better."

"He's beneath you!" Tipton called out.

Maddie ignored him and linked her fingers with Nick's. "Do you want to get ice cream and watch television in bed tonight? I know it's not home, but we can lock the door and tune out the world while pretending it is if you're interested."

Nick grinned, recognizing her bravado for what it was and wanting to encourage it all the same. "That sounds like the best offer I've had all day."

"You and me both."

They turned to leave, several questions unanswered, but their part in this particular tale was done. For both of them, that was the ultimate relief.

Made in United States
Troutdale, OR
12/23/2023

16387571R00119